Jackson ... away from those ... those bewitching blond curls. Mandy could have him forgetting his own name if she half tried.

Maybe she was too good to be true. She had done nothing except do the work for which she'd been hired. No tricks, no flirting, no promising anything she hadn't delivered.

He had to come to terms with his growing awareness of Mandy Parkerson before he could do anything else.

She was an employee only. Nothing more.

But the memory of her sparkling eyes seemed to tease him, the curiosity about how her hair would feel continued to plague him until he could hardly keep his hands to himself.

He wasn't ready to deal with this. Maybe never would be. It was time to focus on the job and keep his distance from Mandy Parkerson and the disturbing thoughts that haunted him whenever he looked at her.

Dear Reader,

Step into warm and wonderful July with six emotional stories from Silhouette Special Edition. This month is full of heart-thumping drama, healing love and plenty of babies!

I'm thrilled to feature our READERS' RING selection, *Balancing Act* (SE#1552), by veteran Mills & Boon and Silhouette Romance author Lilian Darcy. This talented Australian writer delights us with a complex tale of a couple marrying for the sake of their twin daughters, who were separated at birth. The twins and parents are newly reunited in this tender and thought-provoking read. Don't miss it!

Sherryl Woods hooks readers with this next romance from her miniseries, THE DEVANEYS. In *Patrick's Destiny* (SE#1549), an embittered hero falls in love with a gentle woman who helps him heal a rift with his family. Return to the latest branch of popular miniseries, MONTANA MAVERICKS: THE KINGSLEYS, with *Moon Over Montana* (SE#1550) by Jackie Merritt. Here, an art teacher can't help but *moon over* a rugged carpenter who renovates her apartment—and happens to be good with his hands!

We are happy to introduce a multiple-baby-focused series, MANHATTAN MULTIPLES, launched by Marie Ferrarella with *And Babies Make Four* (SE#1551), which relates how a hardheaded businessman and a sweet-natured assistant, who loved each other in high school, reunite many years later and dive into parenthood. *His Brother's Baby* (SE#1553) by Laurie Campbell is the dramatic tale of a woman determined to take care of herself and her baby girl, but what happens when her baby's handsome uncle falls onto her path? In *She's Expecting* (SE#1554) by Barbara McMahon, an ambitious hero is wildly attracted to his new secretary—his new *pregnant* secretary—but steels himself from mixing business with pleasure.

As you can see, we have a lively batch of stories, delivering the very best in page-turning romance. Happy reading!

Sincerely,

Karen Taylor Richman
Senior Editor

Please address questions and book requests to:
Silhouette Reader Service
U.S.: 3010 Walden Ave., P.O. Box 1325, Buffalo, NY 14269
Canadian: P.O. Box 609, Fort Erie, Ont. L2A 5X3

She's Expecting

BARBARA McMAHON

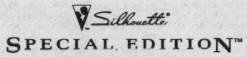

Silhouette®

SPECIAL EDITION™

Published by Silhouette Books

America's Publisher of Contemporary Romance

To Renee and Patti, best friends forever!
Many thanks for always being there.

SILHOUETTE BOOKS

ISBN 0-373-24554-8

SHE'S EXPECTING

Copyright © 2003 by Barbara McMahon

Visit Silhouette at www.eHarlequin.com

Printed in U.S.A.

Books by Barbara McMahon

Silhouette Special Edition

Yours for Ninety Days #1282
Bachelor's Baby Promise #1351
She's Expecting #1554

Silhouette Desire

One Stubborn Cowboy #915
Cowboy's Bride #977
Bride of a Thousand Days #1017
Boss Lady and the Hired Hand #1072
Santa Cowboy #1116
Cinderella Twin #1154
The Older Man #1161
The Cowboy and the Virgin #1215

*Identical Twins!

Silhouette Romance

Sheik Daddy #1132
The Sheik's Solution #1422

BARBARA McMAHON

has made California her home since she graduated from the University of California, Berkeley, way back when! She's convinced she now has the perfect life, living on the western slopes of the Sierra Nevada mountains sipping lattes on her front porch while she watches the deer graze nearby and playing "what if" with different story ideas. Even though she has sold over three dozen books, she says she still has another hundred tales to tell. Barbara also writes for Harlequin Romance. Readers can write Barbara at P.O. Box 977, Pioneer, CA 95666-0777.

WYOMING

NEBRASKA

KANSAS

UTAH

• Fort Collins
• Boulder
★ Denver

• Vail

Pikes Peak
• Colorado Springs

COLORADO

• Grand Junction

Julien

• Durango

N

OKLAHOMA

NEW MEXICO

ARIZONA   All underlined places are fictitious.

Chapter One

"I know he said the place was located in a pristine wilderness, but this is ridiculous!" Mandy Parkerson mumbled aloud as her car continued to barrel along the gravel road. She hadn't seen another vehicle heading in either direction since she'd left the small town of Julian, Colorado, forty minutes ago.

"If they don't do some serious improvement to this road, they'll never have repeat guests. And those who come for the first time might turn around halfway. Especially in winter."

The car bumped and skidded, gravel spewing. The road had obviously been graded at some point, and gravel laid down. But it was already showing ruts from heavy traffic. She didn't even want to speculate what it would be like in rain or a snowstorm. Thank heaven for good weather.

She gripped the steering wheel tighter, easing up on

the accelerator. "Hang on, babykins, it can't be that much farther. He said thirty miles from town, and we've gone at least that."

Six months pregnant, Mandy constantly talked to her baby. She'd read somewhere that children recognized their mother's voice from their time in the womb. So she talked frequently, wanting her infant to know her from the first moment. To know she loved it completely no matter what happened. That she was a mother to be counted on, and she would never desert her child—not as her father had. Or her mother. Or her baby's father.

"At least I think it can't be much farther," she murmured, peering into the distance. It wasn't an easy feat with soaring lodgepole pines lining both sides of the road. The long-range view was where the road cut a swath through the tall timber as it crested a hill. Beyond was the endless blue of a clear autumn sky.

She felt a hint of trepidation as she surveyed the wilderness, but pushed it away. She needed this job. It had sounded perfect when she'd heard about it in the employment agency in Denver—a temporary secretary's position for two months. One that paid almost twice what she'd been earning in the city, with accommodations included. It would tap into her expertise in the building industry, as well. It was the perfect job, even if it was clear across the state from where she lived.

The remote construction site would be in operation only another six to eight weeks before winter closed in and made further work impossible until next spring.

The timing had been perfect. Getting away from Denver had seemed perfect. But now reality began to seep in. Julian was a quaint little mountain town, with one main street and two secondary streets lined with small shops and businesses—and the county's hospital.

Mandy didn't want to forget about medical facilities, not that she expected to need them. She had plenty of time to decide on and settle into a new place before the baby was due. But it didn't hurt to know where the nearest medical assistance was—just in case.

"I sure hope it's not much farther, because if I don't find that construction site soon, I'll have to find a convenient tree!"

One of the definite downsides to pregnancy was the frequent need for rest-room facilities—which weren't available along the side of *this* excuse for a road.

Cresting the hill a few moments later, Mandy slowed, a smile lighting her features. "Hallelujah! Bathroom here we come."

Spread before her was the construction site she'd traveled two hundred miles to reach. Making her way down the sweep of gravel road, she tried to take in everything, from the tall crane swinging a long piling, to the heavy earthmovers parked on the far side of the mammoth clearing, to the sparkling water of the high Alpine lake, part of the spectacular view beyond.

To the left, a hodgepodge of trailers and campers lined the perimeter of the cleared area, with cars and trucks interspersed. Trees surrounded the site, dark green and soaring taller than any she'd seen before. But the jewel was the deep blue Alpine lake, pristine and clear, and stretching as far as the eye could see.

Mandy took a deep breath as she eased her car down the hill. Once the road was paved, the thirty-mile trip from Julian could be made in half the time it had taken her. And it would be a lot smoother.

"We're almost there," she murmured, searching for the office. She'd check in, find out which trailer had been allocated to her, and move in her few things. It wouldn't take long to get settled. She especially wanted to refrigerate the groceries she'd bought in Julian before they spoiled.

And she wanted a bathroom!

She spotted a trailer apart from the others, nearer the work site, and headed for it. It had to be the office. All around her men worked in precision as they toiled to create a luxury resort in the Colorado wilderness. Hard hats gleamed in the sun. The drone of the crane as it swung the piling into place was background noise to the bang of hammers, the whine of a drill and the buzz of saws.

Mandy pulled to a stop by the office. She hastened out of her car and walked up the two steps into the trailer, excitement bubbling inside her.

"Mandy Parkerson! You made it!" Jeff Henshaw rose from behind one of three battered desks. A tall man with a shock of gray hair, he held out his hand. He'd been the one to interview her and offer her the job back in Denver.

Grateful for the friendly welcome, she felt some of her worry fade. Mandy smiled and took his hand. "Your directions were excellent."

"You made good time. I didn't expect you before dark."

"I didn't want to risk driving after sundown on an unfamiliar road. Especially one that isn't paved. Julian looks like a darling town. I stocked up on groceries before I left." She planned to visit on her days off— explore the small shops, eat at the local café, surround herself with some civilization, quiet though it might be.

"It's the closest place for R and R we have when not working. Of course, it's not up to Denver's standards. Come on over and have a seat."

"Uh, maybe I could freshen up first?"

"Go right down that short hall. Take your time. When you're ready, I'll show you around. Get you settled."

"Thanks."

Mandy almost flew down the hall, her long, flowing dress snapping around her legs. She was most comfortable these days in loose-fitting cotton dresses. The pink one she wore now gathered beneath her breasts, the full skirt hitting her midcalf. It swayed when she walked, billowing out behind her as she hurried. It also camouflaged most signs of pregnancy, not that she could be called svelte by any means. But the major growth of her baby was yet to come.

She suddenly wondered how suitable dresses would be on a construction site. It hadn't been a problem in the offices in Denver, but this was definitely not Denver. Still, it wasn't as if she'd be climbing girders or hammering nails.

Mandy was washing her hands when she felt the trailer move slightly, felt a vibration of the floor. Someone had joined Jeff. Was it his partner?

She knew from her interview that Jeff and a man named Jackson Witt had been business partners for several years. And that this was their biggest project to date—and in danger of falling behind because of paperwork snafus.

Not to mention that their previous secretary had quit abruptly, leaving everything in chaos. Mandy hadn't figured out why the secretary had left. Jeff had been quite vague about that, and Mandy hadn't felt it was her place to ask. Now that she was here, and a part of the team, maybe she'd be clued in.

She checked her appearance in the mirror. There

wasn't much she could do about the wild mop of blond curls. They were as tamed as they got. Touching up her pink lipstick, she smiled. Hoping to make as good an impression on Jackson Witt as she had with Jeff, she opened the door and headed back down the short hall. She heard voices and took a deep breath, ready to meet whoever had arrived.

"I saw the car, wanted to meet the new man. There's no emergency on the site." A strong voice carried to her ears.

"I can get the new secretary settled in." That was Jeff's voice. Did it sound a bit hesitant? Mandy wondered.

"Hey, he made good time. There are a few hours left until quitting time. Maybe he can make some headway in that stack of permits today. If we don't get caught up soon, the entire project's going to fall behind schedule, and that's something I don't plan to allow!"

Mandy stepped into the doorway. The man who stood casually beside Jeff's desk, leafing through a stack of mail, was tall, dark, and seemed to seethe with impatience. Mandy blinked. She was five feet two herself, so most men seemed to tower above her. This one had to be six feet tall, with shoulders a yard wide. His T-shirt had the sleeves ripped out, and the rippling muscles covered by taut, tanned skin had her admiring superb musculature. Undoubtedly from hard physical labor. No gym could produce such bronzed skin, defined muscles and the air of command emanating from him even as he glanced through a handful of envelopes.

He caught her movement and looked up. His eyes were dark and unfathomable, but a hint of shock showed. Then they narrowed as he studied her. He looked at Jeff, raising an eyebrow in silent inquiry.

The older man shrugged. "I didn't get around to telling you—our new secretary is a she."

"The hell you say! *You didn't get around to telling me?* You hired her last week! You've been back here four days. Dammit! Jeff, have you gone crazy? The last thing we need around here is a woman. We have fifty-three men working flat out and we need everyone to concentrate on their job, not slack off trying to make time with some blonde! Who knows how much longer we have before the weather turns? Get rid of her!" He tossed the papers on the desk and strode out of the office without looking at Mandy again. The door slammed, the sound reverberating in the narrow confines of the trailer.

"Gee, that went well," Mandy said. She looked at Jeff. "Who was that?" A niggling worry had her guessing exactly who he was.

"That's my partner, Jackson Witt." Jeff smiled wryly. "His bark is worse than his bite. He'll come around."

"I gave up my job, my apartment, and put almost everything I own into storage to come to this job," Mandy said, that hint of trepidation she'd felt earlier expanding, engulfing her. She'd been thrilled to get the position, especially because it was so far from Denver. So thrilled, she'd lost no time in rearranging her life and burning her bridges behind her. If she lost the position before she began, what would she do?

She needed this job!

Jeff rose. "Don't worry about a thing. Jackson'll come around. You're staying. This'll be your desk." He indicated the one near the window—piled with stacks of folders, unopened mail and rolled-up blueprints. Some of the clutter spilled over onto the chair, the wide windowsill behind it and the floor. Had anything been done since the former secretary left? Exactly how long had she—no, undoubtedly *he*—been gone?

"Jackson was right about one thing, though, we need to get going with this paper mess to make sure we stay on target. Pete left us in the lurch when he took off unexpectedly like he did." Jeff looked at her sharply. "I know we discussed timing—two months minimum—but we need to make sure you plan to stay until we shut down for the winter. We need all the paperwork caught up."

"I'm not going anywhere," Mandy said, walking over to the desk to look at the different stacks. She was curious about Jackson Witt, longed to ask some questions about the other partner. How much weight did he carry? Would he try to run her off? Was Jeff able to guarantee she could stay?

Was there more to Jackson Witt's dislike of her than the fact that she was female? Surely Jeff would have taken that into consideration before offering her the job.

And get real—who was going to try to make time with a woman six months pregnant? His workers' concentration was safe!

She wasn't scheduled to start work until tomorrow. Not that she would let that stop her. But first…

"I'd like to put away my groceries. I have some things that need to go into the refrigerator," Mandy said, turning away from the desk. "Then I can begin."

"Tomorrow's soon enough," Jeff said easily.

Mandy studied him a moment. The contrast between the two men was extensive. But she'd better err on the side of caution. "I think it best if I get going today. Sort things out if nothing else." And dig in, hoping to make a place for herself so Mr. Get-Rid-of-Her had to eat his words!

He nodded. "Don't take Jackson's comment to heart. He's a hard man. But as long as you do the job, he'll come around. Come on, I'll show you the trailer. It's the third one in line, next to mine."

When they reached Mandy's car, Jeff nodded toward the row of trailers and campers. "Most of the men stay on-site. A few drive back and forth to town each night. You can park on the far side of the silver trailer."

He crossed the road while she started her car and drove slowly to the trailer indicated. She looked down the long row, wondering how much the command Jackson Witt had issued should concern her. While she couldn't help anyone else's behavior, Jackson Witt had nothing to worry about from her end. She would not encourage flirting. The last thing she wanted was any involvement with another man. Or anyone else, for that matter. She had few friends, but that was by choice. If she didn't let people get close, then she wouldn't be hurt when they deserted her.

She'd been such a fool to trust Marc. Getting involved with him had broken one of her staunchest rules—never date co-workers. But she'd learned that lesson well. Never again!

"One would think," she said aloud, "that after twenty-seven years of being abandoned, let down and disappointed, one would learn. But oh, no, I had to fall for Marc's blue eyes and fancy compliments. Let that be a lesson to you, babykins."

The baby kicked and Mandy smiled, rubbing her stomach gently, her heart swelling with love. "It's you and me, kid. But we'll do great!"

Mandy looked on the new job as a positive sign.

She'd been miserable the last four months at her job in Denver, in the building department where Marc worked as an inspector. Running into each other from time to time was unavoidable. He had totally ignored her since she'd refused to get an abortion. In fact, he seemed to make more of a point to flirt with other women when she was around.

She hadn't been able to turn off her feelings as easily as he had, though by the end of the third week of his rejection, she had grown contemptuous and then angry. Had he had any genuine feelings for her to begin with? She'd once thought he hung the moon. How quickly that illusion had been shattered.

She tried to shake off the feelings of inadequacy that plagued her whenever she thought of that last scene with Marc. He hadn't wanted anything to do with her or their baby. A wife and child had no place in his plans for life.

Had that been how her own father had felt? Was it a man's instinctive reaction to being tied down, to being responsible for another life? Her parents had never been married. Once her father discovered a baby was on the way, he'd taken off fast enough. Mandy could still vaguely remember her mother complaining, before she herself dumped Mandy with social services one day and took off. Mandy had been about five, but still remembered how lost she felt, and how scared.

Yet she saw families all the time—happy families. Fathers who seemed to love their wives and children. Who laughed and smiled during shopping trips to the mall or outings in the park. Even at the building department, some men kept pictures of their families on their desks, had love shining on their faces as they joked about babies teething or waking them in the night.

But the happy family scene seemed to escape Mandy. She'd never mastered it when she was a child, nor found it as an adult. Now she planned a new direction.

The prospect of a good, well-paying job on a site two hundred miles from Denver had given her new hope for the future—a future she planned to build for herself and her child. No more ventures into romance; no more trying to fit in with other people's plans and goals. She would depend on no one but herself! Would make her own decisions and be independent.

The salary offered proved to be much higher than what she'd been earning—higher than usual to attract and hold good workers, the employment agency had told her.

There weren't a lot of amenities. The nearest town was thirty miles away. Nonetheless, the job had seemed heaven-sent, to Mandy. She would mind her own business, keep to herself and save her money like crazy.

As she parked her car, she vowed she'd prove herself to Jeff—and Jackson Witt. They didn't have to worry about their fifty-three other employees. She was here to work and get on with her life, not be a distraction.

Jackson glared at Moose Higgins. The man was one talented crane operator—except when he stopped paying attention. "That's the fourth time I've told you to watch the edge of the cleared space. You just missed whacking those trees. I can't afford to have that crane go out of commission. We're already almost a week behind."

"Hey, boss, lighten up. I didn't hit anything. Came close, but close only counts in horseshoes."

Jackson wasn't appeased. "Don't do it again."

Moose shrugged and set the heavy crane into slow

motion. He was as big as his name implied, but handled the heavy equipment with the delicate skill of a surgeon.

It wasn't Moose's fault, Jackson reluctantly admitted as he watched the skillful man maneuver the huge machine, beginning the intricate process of moving a twenty-five-foot beam into place.

The fault was his. He was angry at Jeff and taking it out on Moose. Dammit, what had his partner been thinking? They were behind on the site work, behind on the paperwork, and already out several thousand dollars, thanks to Pete's embezzlement. To top things off, Jeff had to go hire a petite, feminine *woman!*

It was already September. Before long, the winter snow would start falling, forcing them into a hiatus until spring.

He needed someone who could unjam the logjam, seriously kick some butt and get the local officials off their collective duffs to grant their building approvals. Not some blonde who looked as if a strong wind would knock her over.

This was a hard-core construction site. Men responded to men. Not to some petite blonde with wide blue eyes, dressed in gauzy pink dresses.

Leave it to Jeff to be attracted to a pretty face, hear a sob story and offer her a job, her performance of which would undoubtably set them back even more.

Jackson didn't have time to interview a bunch of people himself. He was needed on-site. Jeff knew that. It was the reason he'd been charged with hiring someone while on the buying trip to Denver. Had he gone crazy, or just been bowled over by bright blue eyes?

Jackson scowled. Blue eyes were blue eyes. He was lucky he'd even noticed the color. She was too young, too small, too feminine to work on a construction site.

He tried to ignore the face that seemed to dance before him as he watched Moose swing the beam. Her sunny smile had dimmed when he'd told Jeff to get rid of her. Her shoulders had slumped slightly for a moment, then straightened up as if she were ready for battle.

Jackson gave a cursory glance around and headed back to the office. There wasn't going to be a battle. He'd told Jeff to send her packing. End of discussion. Now it'd be at least another week before he could interview anyone. He'd better go through the pile on the secretary's desk himself and see what he could handle. Paperwork was not a part of the job he liked, but he'd do it if he had to. And Jeff could do more himself.

It wasn't that his partner didn't pull his weight, but lately Jeff...

Opening the door, Jackson frowned when he saw that the trailer was empty, the phone ringing off the hook. Where was Jeff? Jackson snatched up the phone and looked out the window.

"Witt," he said curtly. He saw the woman's car parked beside the third trailer. What was she doing here? And by the empty trailer?

An uneasy thought sprang to mind. No! Jeff wouldn't—

"Witt, Barton here. We've run into a snafu with your latest lumber order," the voice on the other end said.

Jackson switched gears. He'd deal with the secretary situation after he settled with Miles Barton about the latest problem.

"This'll do fine." Mandy looked around the small trailer. It was like a tiny apartment. The living room segued into a dining nook and galley kitchen. The hallway mimicked the one in the office, leading to a bed and bath.

From one window, she saw the trailer next door. From the back, however, she had a stunning view of the mountains rising majestically around her. And caught a glimmer of the lake.

Best of all, it was free—part of the compensation package. And she still got a healthy salary—how lucky could she be? Jeff's partner was not driving her away from this job!

"I know it's far from the city and all. In your condition, you sure you'll be okay here? The trailers don't have phones, but I'm right next door. And we agreed we'll be shutting down operations for the winter long before you'd start your maternity leave," Jeff said, sounding worried.

Mandy nodded, wanting to pat Jeff's arm and reassure him she was fine. She wasn't used to people taking such an interest and showing so much concern in her life. She'd been on her own since she turned eighteen— nine years ago. It was sweet, but not something she'd grow to expect, or trust.

He was her boss. One of her bosses. And she knew enough not to step over that line.

"This will suit me perfectly."

"I'll bring in your things."

She swiftly put away the perishables, while Jeff helped her put away canned goods and packages. He carried her suitcases and two cardboard boxes into her bedroom.

"I'll unpack later," Mandy told him. She didn't want help unpacking. Or in anything else. The less she depended upon others, the less likely she was to be disappointed when they walked away. ''I'm anxious to get started on the job.''

''Don't you want to rest up after your trip?'' he asked.

''Not necessary. I did nothing but drive, which meant sitting the entire way. Now I'd like to get to work. That's what you're paying me for.'' And she didn't want to provide any reason for his partner to fire her. Despite what Jackson Witt said, she'd come to this job in good faith. He couldn't fire her merely for being a woman. Only if she messed up. Which she didn't plan to do.

Jeff handed her a key as they left the trailer. He watched as Mandy carefully locked her door.

''It's not that we have a lot of crime here,'' he said when they began walking toward the office, ''but with all the men around, you'll need to be a bit careful. Some of these guys are mavericks.''

''I'll keep to myself,'' she said. Her door would not be opened to anyone coming to visit. She wanted time alone and expected to get it.

''Up to walking?'' he asked.

''Sure.'' She smiled, wondering how to set Jeff straight. It couldn't be more than a hundred yards to the office. ''I'm pregnant, not sick. Walking is good exercise. I usually do a couple of miles a day.''

''Not many places to walk around here.''

''Are you kidding? There are hundreds of acres of pristine forest land. Not to mention the shore of the lake. I can't wait to explore that. And if I want a longer ramble, I can always walk back up the road a piece.''

''Not in your condition.'' He looked appalled.

''I'm fine, Jeff.'' She would not allow him to think she couldn't manage on her own. Even if his motives were sincere, she liked her independence. Depending on others always let her down. Besides, she didn't dare let him think she was too fragile to do the job at hand. She needed him on her side if it came to a showdown with his partner.

When Mandy stepped into the office, the first thing she saw was Jackson Witt rummaging through the stacks of papers on her desk. Her heart skipped a beat. In his casual attire, he looked rugged and all male.

Quite a contrast to Marc's rather dapper air. He hated the times he had to inspect the early stages of buildings, especially if the weather was inclement.

Mandy had no difficulty picturing this man out in any and all types of weather, relishing the challenges of nature, defying odds to bring the project in on schedule. While only an inch or two taller than Marc, Jackson radiated a power that the other man would only envy.

"Can I help you find something?" she asked calmly. She knew enough about psychology to know that it would be best to keep any hint of worry from showing.

He turned and looked at her. For a moment Mandy felt a frisson of apprehension. He appeared angry. Or was that scowl his perpetual expression?

"Why are you still here? We'll pay for your travel time and any inconvenience we caused. You might want to take off before it gets dark."

"There has been no inconvenience. I've come to work and I'll do my job." She walked behind the desk and sat down defiantly, almost holding her breath as she threw out the challenge. Jeff remained by the door—in order to make a quick escape? Mandy wondered.

"Are you *pregnant?*" Jackson asked in disbelief, staring at her stomach.

Had he not noticed earlier?

"Almost six months. Don't worry, it's not contagious. And it doesn't interfere with my abilities."

He swung around to Jeff. "You hired a *pregnant woman* to come out here? I don't believe this! Have you lost what little mind you had left?"

"She's got experience in the building industry. Her skills are great. She'll be able to do a lot to help out without our having to teach her every step. She'll be doing office work, not heavy construction. Besides, it wasn't as if we had a lot of choice. People aren't exactly champing at the bit to come to some construction site thirty miles from the nearest town—even for a couple of months. I figured any help was better than coming back empty-handed."

Mandy looked at Jeff in dismay. She'd been sure her experience had impressed him, that he'd truly thought she was the best person for the job. The pride she'd felt in landing the position deflated.

Standing suddenly, she tilted her head pugnaciously. "Give me a week. If you aren't totally satisfied with all I've done, I'll leave and you won't even have to pay me for the work," she said before she could think.

Jackson looked at her, frowning.

Jeff looked at her, frowning.

"No." Jackson's flat-out denial was immediate; no compromise from him. His dark eyes sent a shiver coursing down her back. Mandy wanted more than anything to prove to him she could do the job—to have him change his mind and eat crow.

"That's not fair to you, Mandy," Jeff protested.

"I think it's fair. Especially if you *are* satisfied with my work, I stay and you give me a bonus." It was a gamble, but she was desperate. Her gaze locked with

Jackson's and endless moments ticked by. He was the one to convince.

"Today is Tuesday. You have until Friday. Then you're gone," Jackson said, breaking eye contact first. He turned and glared at Jeff. "And I'll do the interviewing next time."

"Won't be a next time," Mandy muttered, already delving into the stack of rolled-up blueprints.

She continued to sort and stack the various documents on her desk, almost holding her breath until the two men left. Then with a whoosh, she let it out, leaning back in her chair and gazing around her in dismay.

What had she so recklessly done? She'd be lucky to find her way around the office by Friday, much less prove to be invaluable to a man whose mind was made up that she was expendable.

She needed the money. How foolish to say they needn't pay her. Her primary reason for accepting a job so far away from everything she knew was the added pay. She didn't have much in savings, though she'd been scrimping to augment what she had ever since she'd discovered she was pregnant. Ever since she'd learned Marc wanted nothing further to do with her or their child.

Something about Jackson Witt got her back up and gave her a new focus. She wanted him to turn around and admit she was suitable for the job. It was personal now.

The baby kicked and Mandy idly rubbed her stomach. "Buckle up, babykins, we're in for a bumpy ride!"

The phone rang and Mandy answered it. Her job had begun in earnest.

By the time Mandy's stomach had growled for the third time, she was ready to call it a day. Glancing out the window, she noticed all was quiet on the job site. The noise from the heavy machinery had faded long ago. The sound of hammers ringing and the buzz of the saws had ended without her noticing.

She surveyed her desk with quiet satisfaction. She'd gone through everything and sorted it into piles. She had fielded calls, settled one problem with a vendor and been the target of curious construction workers who had found one dumb excuse after another to stop into the office during the afternoon.

Jeff had been there most of the time. She'd done her best to ignore the visitors, claiming she hadn't a clue yet where things were when they asked, and suggesting they talk to Jackson. She'd love to know if any had followed through. She could just imagine what Jackson Witt would have said to any man who mentioned he'd talked with her!

Though she hoped none were crazy enough to ask him. She didn't want anyone giving credence to his prediction about her being a distraction.

Mandy walked outside, locking the door behind her. The fresh air was pleasant, though cool. The sun had already moved behind the ridge, bathing the valley in deep shadows.

When she drew near her trailer, her relief was almost tangible. She was on her own until eight the next morning.

The door of the first trailer opened and Jackson stepped out. His eyes narrowed as he saw her, but he said nothing, walking on down the beaten path toward the lake as if she hadn't been there.

She tossed her head. She didn't care. He could be as rude as he liked when they weren't working. It was only for two months and she could stand anything for that long.

Tonight she'd unpack, take a soothing bath and fix something light for dinner. Then it was bed for her! She'd read until she fell asleep. It had been a long day.

Dammit, it was bad enough having Mandy Parkerson work here, but Jeff had to make it convenient for her to stay on-site. The whole setup was explosive. Jackson knew trouble in the making. He only hoped he could stave it off until she left on Friday.

Jackson headed for the lake, and the quiet spot he liked to find at the end of the day.

One of the trailers had lights on inside. It wasn't dark, but the sun had already slipped behind the high peaks to the west. Twilight fell early in the high country in late September.

He liked this time of day. He always had. He and his late wife, Sara.

As he walked to the lake's edge, he heard the drone of television coming from a couple of trailers, ribald conversation from another. A small group of guys sat in folding chairs near one camper, swapping stories. When Jackson reached the lake, he nodded to a couple of men trying their hand at fishing.

They were building a luxury resort for the Wind-haven Corporation in the middle of the Colorado wilderness. The lake was one of the major attractions. The proximity to cross-country ski resorts and hunting and fishing were other aspects the corporation planned to highlight. As well as a state-of-the-art spa to attract women.

For a place to relax, it wouldn't be beat. Jackson knew the resort would charge guests an arm and a leg, and visitors would happily pay for the remote luxury and pristine setting.

He'd be long gone by then. To another site, another job. Another couple of years in a remote location. Getting through life one day at a time.

He walked along the edge of the lake, stopping at a tree that had fallen partially into the water. Placing a foot on the trunk, he rested his elbow against his knee and took a swig of the cold soft drink he'd carried. He was alone and liked it that way.

Sara would have loved this place, he thought for the hundredth time.

The familiar ache took hold. He always missed her, but especially at twilight. They'd made it a tradition to have a quiet drink together, just the two of them, before dinner every evening. Even after Sammy had come along, it had been their special time to talk over their respective days, and to be with each other. To shut out the rest of the world and draw their own world around them.

He gripped the can tightly. The ache would get worse as the night wore on. It had been three years, but it could have been three minutes or three decades. With his wife gone it was like a part of himself had been amputated. Which it had—the best part of him.

He could close his eyes and see her—tall and slim with dark eyes and sleek dark hair that cupped her head. She'd been almost as tall as he was when she'd worn high heels. They'd know each other since second grade. Their likes had meshed; their thoughts had run parallel. Their dreams had been the same.

God, the ache was impossible. Some days he thought he couldn't make it without her. Her and Sammy.

If he closed his eyes, he could see her walking toward him. Hear her sweet voice—

"Mr. Witt, there's a problem with my water. I can't find Jeff. Can you fix it?"

Jackson opened his eyes and turned. Instead of Sara's dark beauty, he confronted the petite blonde Jeff had hired. The petite, *pregnant* blonde who barely came up to his shoulder.

Irritation rose. What did she want now? If she thought he planned to baby-sit her until Friday, she had another thought coming. He still didn't know why he'd given her until Friday. She should have headed back to Julian already.

Chapter Two

"What do you want?"

"Someone to fix the water in my trailer. I knocked on Jeff's door. He said he has the trailer next door to mine, but he's not there. And I don't know anyone else to ask. I certainly don't want you to think I was *flirting* with someone if I asked for assistance," Mandy said.

Jackson took another swallow of the soda, his cherished quiet shattered. He scanned her from head to toe, irritated anew at the sight of her. The asperity in her voice was noticeable. He straightened. She was right; if there was a problem, he or Jeff should fix it. No sense opening a crack in a door for any of the men to think it was an invitation.

"What's wrong with the water?"

"I can't get any hot. It comes out cold from both faucets. There's a hot-water heater, but I don't know a thing about it and don't know if it's working properly."

"Probably needs a new propane tank hooked up."

She stared at him. Her eyes were darker in the twilight—not deep brown as Sara's had been, but navy blue.

Navy blue eyes? It had to be lack of light, or altitude sickness. What was wrong with him? She had plain old blue eyes, period.

He sighed over the inevitable and turned to begin to walk back along the shore, then up the slight incline, heading toward the trailers. Despite not wanting her around, he would fix the blasted hot-water heater. A pregnant woman needed warm water.

A shaft of pain pierced him. He remembered how much Sara had liked soaking in hot baths when she'd been pregnant with Sammy. Sometimes he'd joined her, the two of them sloshing water everywhere.

Quickening his pace, he tried to put distance between him and the memories. It took a couple of minutes to realize Mandy Parkerson was almost running to keep up with him.

Jackson stopped abruptly. She skidded to a halt and looked at him, her breasts rising and falling rapidly as she tried to catch her breath. The higher elevation took some getting used to. Exertion wasn't recommended until a person had become acclimated.

"You needn't run," he said.

"I want to see how you fix the hot-water heater. If there's a problem in the future, I can take care of it myself if I know how."

"There won't be another problem before Friday."

She tilted her chin, meeting his gaze. "I meant beyond Friday—when I'm still here and a valuable member of the team!"

Jackson felt a twitch of amusement. He'd give her

credit for being tenacious, if nothing else. But the proof would be in the work and the way she handled herself. He didn't have time for dilettantes. Tomorrow he'd make sure she realized fully what all was involved. He'd bet she'd be gone by sundown.

He turned back toward her trailer, moving more slowly, conscious of the woman beside him. He'd never had to shorten his stride with Sara.

As they walked along, Jackson's senses were teased by the floral scent that seemed to float around Mandy Parkerson. It was light and delicate—like she was. It brought home how much he'd missed a woman's presence in the last three years. And how long the years stretched out, empty and lonely, ahead of him.

Unable to bear the reality of Sara's and Sammy's deaths, he'd thrown himself into his work, taking on more and more. Joining Jeff in partnership, he had pushed to build their newly formed J&J Construction to the size it was today. He didn't have time for friendships beyond the job site, and had no plans to ever get involved with another woman. One heartache in this lifetime was more than he could handle.

Yet for the first time in three years, he was actually looking at a woman. Smelling her scent. Speculating about the true color of her eyes. And wishing she were a hundred miles away.

Innocently walking beside him, Mandy obviously hadn't a clue about the turmoil he felt. The sooner he got her hot-water heater fixed, the sooner she'd be closed up in her trailer and out of sight—and scent. He didn't need her to remind him of all he'd lost.

It took five minutes to locate a new propane tank, hook it to the hot-water heater and ignite the pilot light. Once he heard the whoosh that indicated the heater was working, he turned and almost crashed into her. Mandy had been at his elbow every step of the way, watching closely as he worked, asking intelligent questions.

She stepped back quickly, a hint of worry in her eyes.

"It'll take a while for the water to heat," he said, wanting to step back, to put distance between them. But the close confines of the trailer didn't allow that luxury. Why didn't she move?

"I know. I'll eat dinner first. Then take a quick shower." She sighed softly. "I had been hoping for a nice hot bath, but a shower is all this place has." She smiled politely and stepped back into the living area of the trailer.

Jackson followed, intent on leaving before he did something else stupid. He had a tub in his trailer—the only one in camp, if he remembered correctly. For an instant he almost offered her the use of it. Then sanity took hold. He didn't want her here, and didn't plan to do anything to encourage her staying. By Friday, she'd have to admit defeat, and depart.

And if life wasn't as comfortable as she'd hoped, maybe she'd leave even earlier.

"We start work at eight," he said gruffly, feeling a hint of guilt for denying her such a minor bit of comfort. But he was determined to have her gone in three days.

"I'll be there. Thank you for fixing the heater."

She ushered him to the door and practically shut it in his face.

He stood on the step for a moment, surprised by her move. *What did you expect?* he asked himself as he walked away. He had done nothing since they'd met to encourage any friendly feelings. Still, he admitted he had expected her to try to change his mind—with a smile, or soft words, or an invitation for a drink. The fact that she hadn't surprised him.

Mandy stood beneath the hot shower some time later and reveled in the warmth. She wished she could have had a nice soak, but the water felt almost as good cascading down as it would sitting in it. Tilting back her head, she wet her hair, relishing the feeling. She wished the lake was warm enough to swim in—not that late September was the time to go swimming in Colorado's high country. The lake was probably icy cold even in summer. But it had looked inviting.

When the water began to turn cool, she shut it off and stepped out into the minuscule bathroom. It didn't take long to dry off and don the flannel nightie she'd brought. Nights were cool in Denver, and she'd known they would be cold in the mountains. Combing her hair, she debated using a dryer. Her hair would curl in any case, so she might as well let it dry naturally.

Slipping beneath the covers a little while later, she turned off the light without reading. She wanted to get a good night's sleep. She had a feeling she'd need all her wits about her tomorrow to prove to at least one critical partner that she was the perfect secretary.

Curiously, she had no doubt that if she proved her worth, Jackson would let her stay until they closed down for the winter. She suspected he was an honorable man, a man of his word.

She grinned in the darkness. He hadn't wanted to help her tonight. But he had. Without a word of complaint. Another man might have said that was one hardship of working on a remote site—that they all dealt with cold showers—as a way to discourage her. But he hadn't.

He'd been patient in answering her questions, too, though he was convinced she would never need a working knowledge of the heater or propane tank.

Would he graciously accept defeat when she showed him she could stay the course? Or would he always be looking for fault, searching for any excuse to fire her and get rid of the woman secretary? He'd agreed to the outrageous terms she'd flung out. If she passed, she'd stay. Something about the man told her that. But he was the one who'd decide if she passed, and she knew the deck was stacked against her.

Mandy was already on the phone to the county building department when Jackson entered the trailer the next morning. She'd seen him up on the framework of the main building when she'd crossed to the office, but he hadn't seen her. He'd been deep in conversation with two other men, comfortably at home on the high skeleton of the new resort. How long had he worked in construction? Probably since he was a teenager, to be so comfortable on precarious structures.

He looked at her with surprise when he entered.

"It's only a few minutes past eight o'clock. If he could be here by one, that would work," she said to the woman on the other end of the line.

Mandy tried to focus on the conversation at hand, ignoring Jackson's presence to the best of her abilities. But something about him sparked an awareness she wasn't used to. It was as if the air shimmered with static electricity in his presence.

She almost grinned at her frivolous thoughts. If there were electricity present, he'd use it to zap her away.

Mandy smiled in triumph, but let none of her jubilation show in her voice when the woman on the other end acquiesced. "Thank you, I'll let them know he'll be here by one."

She hung up the phone.

"That was?" Jackson asked, leaning against the edge of his desk, his concentration on her. His dark eyes were narrowed, offering no clue to his feelings, yet the intensity was disconcerting. Mandy felt almost as if he touched her. A tangible awareness seemed to grow. Shivering slightly, she tried to ignore her reactions, and smiled in delight.

"The county building department. You'll have an inspector here by one." She wanted to jump up and dance around in triumph, but contained her excitement. Jeff had told her how frustrated they'd been with inspection delays. Let Jackson think it was all in a day's work for someone with her expertise. A few more triumphs like that and he'd have to admit she was more than suitable—she was indispensable!

"And just how did you manage that feat?" His eyes never left hers as he awaited her answer.

"Knowing who to contact and how to apply the right pressure." And a lot of luck, but he didn't have to know that part.

He stared at her for a long moment. Mandy caught her breath, held it as her heart rate sped up exponentially. She couldn't look away, couldn't break contact, could only gaze into those dark eyes that gave nothing away. What was he thinking? Did he feel any of the shimmering tension that seemed to fill the office trailer?

Abruptly, he nodded once and moved to sit behind his desk. The phone rang and he snatched it up.

She glanced away, slowly letting her breath out and taking another. What had just happened?

She drew a line through that item on her to-do list,

trying to focus on all she had to accomplish and not on the other occupant of the office. Getting the inspector out on such short notice was a small victory in the greater scheme of things, but it definitely didn't hurt that Mr. Doubting Thomas over there had witnessed it. Chalk one up for her side.

Now if she could only ignore him and the strange reactions she experienced, maybe she could get something else crossed off her lengthy list.

Despite the edge of tension that seemed to permeate the office during the morning, Mandy was able to accomplish a great deal. But even as she diligently worked through the backed-up paperwork, she was conscious of Jackson Witt more than she should have been.

The way he ran his fingers through that thick hair had nothing to do with anything, and she had no business noting the gesture each time he made it. His hair was almost black, and thick. When he ran his fingers through it, it looked mussed. Sexy.

She blinked and stared back at her notes. Don't go there!

The sound of his deep voice when speaking on the phone did not send shivers down her back. That was the draft from the door, she tried to convince herself. But the words before her blurred as she imagined him holding her close and speaking softly in her ear.

When he frowned at something, she was glad that glare was not directed at her, but her heart rate picked up, anyway. And she wondered what he'd look like if he smiled, or laughed.

Jeff joined them at ten, after reviewing plans with one of the masons on the far side of the site. His presence eased the tension a notch or two. Maybe with a third person there, her wild imagination would ease up and she could get something accomplished.

But Mandy couldn't completely relax. She was too aware on a sensual level of the man at the adjacent desk. Did Jackson normally stay in the office all day? Wasn't he needed on the construction site to oversee something? Had he only stayed in the office today to keep an eye on her—hoping to find fault and get rid of her even earlier than Friday?

She'd go crazy if he spent eight hours a day, every day, in such close proximity.

"It's after twelve. When do you plan to eat lunch?" Jackson said unexpectedly.

Mandy looked up from the stack of invoices she was trying to put in order. She glanced at her watch. The morning had flown by.

"Is this the normal lunch hour?"

He nodded.

Silence outside indicated the men had stopped work.

She rose, smoothing her dark blue dress and taking her purse. "I'll be back at one, then."

"If I'm not here, follow up on these calls, will you?" he asked, holding out a small stack of pink telephone messages.

"Certainly."

Jeff smiled, keeping his face down as if studying the blueprints spread across his desk.

Jackson glanced at him. "Something funny?"

His partner looked up and shook his head. "Thought you didn't want Mandy here. You delegating work to her now?"

"If she were staying, she'd need to be able to handle the office when you and I aren't here. Might as well see how she shapes up while we are still around."

A hint of exhilaration swept through Mandy as she walked back to her trailer. Was Jackson thawing, as Jeff had predicted? One gesture wasn't enough to judge. A cordial word or two would help. Was he as gruff with all his employees? Maybe he wasn't used to being around a woman.

Not that she wanted special consideration.

After she prepared her lunch, she sat down on the sofa and put her feet up on a chair. Leaning back, she enjoyed being able to totally relax. She was tired—not that she'd admit that to her boss. She'd give anything if she could take a short nap.

Instead, she nibbled on her tuna sandwich, idly speculating about the taciturn Jackson Witt.

He seemed a hard man, with definite opinions and not much give in him. How had he and easygoing Jeff ever hooked up? He was years younger than Jeff, in his early thirties, she'd guess, while Jeff had to be in his mid- to late fifties. Did Jackson ever smile? She hadn't seen him do so yet. Not that they'd spent that much time together. And, truth to tell, she didn't mind if they didn't spend any more time together. Until she could convince him she was the best person for the job, he was the enemy.

Ordinarily, she'd be pleased with what she'd accomplished with little direction on her first day. Still, she knew it might not be enough to suit him. He had the final say. But she'd go down fighting every inch of the way!

Jackson glanced up when, promptly at one o'clock, Mandy reentered the office. He nodded briefly and returned to scheduling the rotation for next week's workload, trying to ignore her. Not an easy task.

Jackson was growing intrigued with the new secretary. He'd expected her to flounce around, ask a ton of questions, flirt with anything in jeans and play at office work.

So far the delicate-looking blonde had succeeded in getting an inspector out on a couple of hours' notice, had organized the mess of her desk and not flirted once. She ignored the men who stopped by with one excuse or another. Was she playing some game, or was she for real?

He stared at her as she glanced through the phone messages he'd handed her earlier. After brushing back her blond mane, she picked up the phone and dialed the first number. She deliberately put a smile on her face, staring at the note in hand. He frowned. What was she doing? Following up on problems was nothing to smile about.

And were those curls and waves natural? Must be. With the impatient way she brushed them out of her way, it was unlikely they were a perm gone wrong.

Blond covered a variety of hues. Her hair was a mixture of gold, wheat-white and honey tumbling across her shoulders. Maybe she should have cut it like Sara's, short and sleek. Or would those curls persist? Did they feel as soft and silky as they looked? Would they wrap around a man's fingers if he threaded his hands through them?

He glanced away. What the hell was he doing, speculating about a woman's hair? He rose and slammed out of the office, disgust warring with frustration. He'd told Jeff that having a woman secretary was a bad idea.

Before he could decide whether to head for home to grab a bite to eat, check out what Jeff was up to, or make sure Moose wasn't hotdogging with the crane,

Jackson spotted the county car descending the sweep of road leading to the site.

Taking a deep breath, he forced his mind on the upcoming inspection. He refused to think about Mandy Parkerson and her wild mop of curls. Or her blue eyes. Or her damned sunny smile. She'd be gone by Friday.

Jackson didn't return to the office during the afternoon. Mandy took advantage of the opportunity to question Jeff. Getting a better picture of the operation would go a long way in bringing her up to speed. The atmosphere was much more relaxed, for which she was grateful.

There were phone calls to field, files to search for, and other routine tasks, in addition to trying to catch up with the work that had piled up since the former secretary had left. But Mandy still asked questions, tried to make sense of where they stood and how much they were trying to complete before winter.

By five she was glad to call it a day. It had been hectic, but exhilarating work. And she was making progress. Now she would change into something comfortable and take a short walk before dinner. Another early night was on the schedule. She suspected it'd take a couple of days to get used to the hectic pace, in addition to the catch-up she needed to do.

Her doctor had told her to expect to grow tired more easily. How right she'd been.

Calling good-night to Jeff, Mandy headed for her trailer.

Two men lounged by the office steps when she descended.

"Evening, ma'am," one said.

She smiled and nodded, but kept walking.

They fell into step with her.

"Welcome to Windhaven's future newest resort," one said. "Or it will be when we're finished here. I'm Bill Frates. This here's Tim Harris."

"How do you do? I'm Mandy Parkerson." She kept her pace brisk. It was nice of them to introduce themselves, but she wasn't planning to become a good buddy to anyone. She'd do her job and keep to herself.

"It gets lonely eating dinner by yourself," Bill said. "Want to join us tonight?"

Mandy increased her pace just a bit. "Thanks for the offer, but I have plans." Only a few more yards to her trailer and safety. She resisted looking around to see if Jackson was watching her. He would surely consider this distracting his men.

"Tomorrow night then?"

"I'll have to see." She reached for her key and unlocked her door.

"It was nice meeting you both," she said politely. Stepping inside, she closed the door and leaned against it for a moment. That was not distracting the men, as Jackson had direly foretold. But it might come close. Too bad they didn't know she had no plans to get involved with anyone—even on a superficial level!

Marc's cruel defection had cured her of romantic notions. Some people were destined for happy ever after. She wasn't one of them.

She'd finally learned that lesson. She knew she had nothing to offer a man. Her own father had run out on her mother before she'd been born. Marc had turned away once he heard about the baby. He'd found her fun to date for a while, but commitment hadn't been in his plans. Not to the baby, and especially not to her.

She patted her tummy. "Whoever you are, sweetie,

I'll love you forever,'' she whispered, an overwhelming glow of love swelling. She would cherish her child and never abandon it, no matter what the hardships.

Not as her parents had abandoned her.

As the baby grew and developed, so did her love for her unborn child. Mandy wondered how her mother could have carelessly left her own daughter in foster care. Had she ever regretted forsaking her only child? Mandy had been five when her mother had dumped her with social services, claiming she was unable to manage anymore.

Mandy had made up tales when she was younger—about how her mother really adored her, but because she had no money, had had to reluctantly give her up to foster care, temporarily.

Then, in true melodramatic fashion, she had died, leaving Mandy to languish in the system until she turned eighteen.

Of course, once she was older, Mandy had figured out it was more likely her mother just hadn't wanted to be bothered. That she had found it easier to deal with life unencumbered by an unwanted child.

The old sorrows surfaced again and Mandy pushed them away. It was all ancient history.

Her child would have all the love and devotion from its mother she could give it. And she had enough for two—to make up for Marc's defection. She would not let history repeat itself!

Soon she would no longer be alone—she'd have her precious baby. They'd be a happy, close family of two.

Less than ten minutes later, Mandy peeked out her door. She'd put on loose shorts, a cotton top and a light sweatshirt. It was growing cooler by the minute, with the sun already behind the western peaks. But once she began walking she'd warm up.

No one appeared to be paying any attention to her. She locked her door and glanced around. Down by the lake a group of men were laughing and talking. Closer to her trailer, she saw four or five men near one of the campers, leaning back in camp chairs, shooting the breeze.

Taking a deep breath, she stepped out briskly. She waved when they called greetings, but didn't stop as she passed the group near the camper. Walking briskly, she headed for the lake. If she skirted the group there, she could head to the right and walk along the shore for a while.

If felt great to be outside after a day cooped up in the office. The air was scented with pine and a hint of fresh lake water. The dirt beneath her feet was so dry it puffed in little clouds as she walked. Her shoes would be covered in red dust by the time she got back.

The group by the lake grew quieter as she drew near. Circling around them, she once again smiled and waved. One man looked as if he planned to join her, but hesitated. She refused to make eye contact, and hoped it would indicate she was not interested in companionship.

Small waves rippled quietly against the narrow beach. In spring, she suspected, the water rose to the tree line. But by late summer, the level had dropped, so there was plenty of room to walk on the compacted soil.

Striding quickly along, Mandy smiled with delight. It was the perfect ending to the day. She would make a habit of this. The water lapped gently at the shore. Wind rustled softly in the pines. By walking briskly, she kept warm, though she did slip on her sweatshirt. Maybe jeans would have been more suitable.

Before she'd gone too far, however, she was breathing hard. She couldn't be that out of shape—she'd been walking a couple of miles after work every day in Denver. And the elevation here wasn't that much higher, was it?

By the time Mandy decided to turn back, she was feeling decidedly queasy. Spots danced before her eyes and she was gasping for breath. A sharp pain pierced her head. She slowed her pace, anxious now only to return to the trailer and lie down.

Eyeing a fallen log near the lake, she considered sitting to rest for a moment, but pushed on. The light was fading fast. She needed to return to the trailer.

Once again she saw the men gathered near the water when she rounded the bend. Several were fishing. The others were drinking and laughing, unwinding after a tough day.

She stumbled, reached out to catch herself before she could fall. Then everything went black.

Chapter Three

"Hey, boss, come quick. We've got a problem!" Bill Frates stopped running as soon as he spotted Jackson.

Jackson frowned and rose from where he'd been sitting beside the lake. This had better be good. The men knew the unwritten rule: don't bother the boss at twilight.

"What's wrong?" He quickly covered the distance between himself and Bill.

"It's the new secretary. She fell and is unconscious."

Jackson picked up his pace. "How did she fall?" he asked. A sudden stab of fear struck him. She was all right, wasn't she? There was nothing wrong with her baby, was there? They were a half hour or more from Julian. Did the town have a helicopter for emergency airlifts?

Bill turned and hurriedly led the way back along the lake.

"She was just walking. A bunch of us were by the lake—you know how Tim and Sonny love fishing. We were all hanging out. So when she came into view, we watched her. Then she just dropped like a rock."

"Damn!" Jackson saw the crowd of men. He began to run.

The men parted so Jackson could get to the center of the group. Tim knelt beside her, gently shaking her shoulder and calling her name.

There on the ground lay Jackson's new secretary. Her blond hair spread around her like a nimbus, highlighting the rusty-brown color of the ground. Her legs were bent, her arms outstretched. Her eyes were closed and her chest rose and fell quickly.

Jackson swallowed hard and stooped down.

"Mandy?" He shook her gently. He glanced around. "Did she trip on something? Who saw her fall?"

"A lot of us, boss," Tom Harmon said. "We were all watching her walk along, speculating if she'd speak to us on her way back, when she seemed to stumble, then just crumpled up. She didn't hit hard. We didn't see any rocks around." The ground was strewn with a thick carpet of pine needles, which would have softened the hard-packed earth.

Jackson gently patted her cheek. "Mandy, wake up."

Her breathing was rapid and her color pale. He didn't know what was wrong, but whatever it was, it was worse because she was pregnant.

Slipping his arms beneath her shoulders and knees, he rose, holding her against her chest.

"Someone find Jeff and have him call for an ambulance," Jackson said, heading toward the trailers. She didn't weigh a thing. Was she too thin? Against one arm, he could feel the softness of the skin beneath her

knees. Her head was nestled on his shoulder, her fragrance swirling around him.

Ignoring the tingling tendrils of awareness, Jackson
pushed through the group and began the ascent to the
trailers.

She stirred and opened her eyes, blinking a couple of
times as she tried to get oriented.

"What happened?" She looked up into Jackson's
face.

"You took a tumble. Knocked yourself out, I think,"
he replied.

She rubbed her forehead with one hand and struggled.
"Put me down. I can walk."

"We'll wait for the paramedics to determine that."

"I don't need paramedics. I'm fine. Put me down."

"Jeff's calling an ambulance. You'll be in Julian in
no time."

"I'm not going to Julian. I'm fine!" She pushed
against his shoulder. "Really, Jackson, this is embarrassing. Please, put me down."

He stopped. The group of men trailing behind him
stopped. Slowly he set her on her feet, keeping his arm
around her shoulders, watching for any sign of weak-
ness.

Mandy drew a deep breath and clutched his free arm.
"I do feel a bit wobbly, but that's all. If I can just sit
down, I'll be fine. Really, no paramedics."

He glanced at one of the men and nodded toward the
office. "Catch Jeff, tell him to hold off on the ambulance for the time being."

"Forever," Mandy muttered, glancing around. Color
rose in her face. "Good grief," she murmured softly,
"is the entire crew here?"

"I don't know who's here and who's not. It doesn't

matter. Let's get you to your trailer. Then I want some answers.''

They walked slowly, silently, to her trailer. She clung to his arm, but walked without other assistance. Behind them, the men began to disperse, until only Jackson and Mandy walked up to her steps. She dug her key from her pocket and inserted it. She opened the door, and he followed her in before she could protest.

Twice now she'd interrupted his evening routine. Did she plan to make a habit of it? He scowled. He knew she'd be trouble.

''I'm fine. Thanks for the rescue,'' she said, sinking down on her sofa. She leaned back and closed her eyes, her hands resting protectively on her stomach. How was it he seemed to take all the air from the room? He towered over her and she kept her eyes closed to establish a modicum of control over the situation.

''What happened?'' His voice was grim.

''I don't know. I was taking a walk. Then the next thing I knew, you were carrying me up the hill.'' She opened her eyes and looked at him. ''No small feat these days.''

He rubbed the back of his neck. ''You didn't trip on anything?''

''No, but I have a piercing headache. I had it before I blacked out. I don't think I hit my head on anything.''

''Altitude sickness, maybe?''

''Shouldn't be. I walk all the time in Denver.''

''Which is several thousand feet lower in elevation. It takes a while to get acclimated to the high country.''

''Noted.''

''You're a liability here, Mandy Parkerson. Not only to the job, but to yourself. What if you'd been injured? How long would it take an ambulance to get here?

You're risking your own safety and that of your baby. You'll have to leave. We'll pay you for the week.''

She flew to her feet and glared at him, her hands clenching into fists on her hips. ''Now just a minute here, Jackson Witt. You can't fire me for falling on my own time. I'm not hurt. Thank you for your concern, but I was hired to work for your company, and if you fire me for some trumped-up, bogus reason I'll sue you up one side and down the other!''

''A cheap price to pay—at least I'll know you and your baby are safe. It's too dangerous here for someone in your condition. I don't want anyone hurt. If you won't think about yourself, at least consider your child!'' He glared at her for a long moment, then spun around and left.

Mandy slowly sank back onto the sofa, her knees weak as wet spaghetti. What had that been about? It almost sounded as if he cared about her safety. Or was it only to minimize any liability to his precious construction site?

''Jackson, what's going on? Is she all right?'' Jeff hurried over from the office, his face creased with worry.

Jackson nodded. ''She fell. I think she fainted. It's not uncommon in pregnant women. And we're at a higher elevation from Denver. I think she overextended herself. She claims she's fine, but she's history. Get rid of her, Jeff. You hired her, you fire her. She's a danger to herself and that baby.'' He strode off, angry with the woman for taking risks. Angry that he even cared.

The ache that took hold wouldn't let go. Sara had never taken risks. She'd been careful her entire life— especially so when pregnant with Sammy.

And in the end, it hadn't mattered. It hadn't been enough.

But to deliberately take a risk when a child was involved was unacceptable. He wouldn't be a party to it!

Jeff knocked on the trailer door. Mandy answered immediately.

"Hi, Jeff, come in." Stepping back, she smiled wryly. "I guess you heard."

"I came to see if you're all right."

"Honestly, I don't know what happened. One minute I'm walking along, the next…" The next she knew she'd been swept into the strongest pair of arms she'd ever felt. Jackson had carried her up the incline from the lake as if she'd weighed nothing.

She could still feel the strength of his arms, the muscles of his chest. She couldn't ever remember anyone so strong, anyone who handled her so gently.

The special male scent that radiated from his skin seemed to linger and cause all sorts of reactions, just as it had in the office earlier. The heat that had enveloped her when she realized he was carrying her made her act silly. Once in the safety of her trailer, she had lashed out in retaliation—and made an idiot of herself in the process. He'd only been watching out for her safety. There was nothing personal in his concern; he probably felt that way with all his employees.

She swallowed and sat down again, knees definitely wobbly. Should she listen to his advice? Leave when she'd just arrived—without even proving how competent she was? She couldn't do that. She had too much riding on this job.

"Guess I tried too much. Jackson suggested I'm suffering from altitude sickness. Can I use the phone in the office to call my doctor? Just to check in?''

"I can take you to the hospital in Julian," Jeff said instantly.

"Maybe, but first I'll check in with my regular obstetrician. I've heard of pregnant women fainting—although it's never happened to me before. Maybe Jackson is right and it's just a reaction to the higher altitude. Which means I'll have to take it easy until I get used to being at this elevation. But I need to get some exercise. I can't just sit at a desk all day."

"Are you sure you don't want me to run you into town to be checked by a doctor?"

"Let me check in with mine first."

Jeff escorted her to the office, which was miraculously empty. Thankfully, Mandy sat behind her desk, glad she didn't have to face Jackson again so soon. She dialed the phone and spoke to the answering service, leaving her number. Hanging up, she looked at Jeff.

"They'll track the doctor down for me. I'll just wait here until she calls back. Don't let me keep you from anything. I'm feeling fine, truly. I'm not going to keel over. Even my headache is fading."

"I'll sit with you. Maybe Jackson was right. Maybe this is too much to expect of a pregnant woman," Jeff said thoughtfully.

"Don't you start! We'll find out what happened and see it doesn't happen again. I need this job, Jeff. Please don't fire me." She hated having to plead to keep her job, but she could understand how, after this, they were uncertain she could last.

He looked uneasy. "I don't know if this will work, Mandy."

"It will." She wished she felt as confident as she had

the day before. Had she placed the doubt in Jeff's mind? She needed his support!

He settled in behind his desk, leaning back in his chair, his feet on the desk as they waited for the doctor's call. "Are you going back to Denver when the baby comes, or are you originally from somewhere else?" he asked.

"I have no family and no ties to Denver." Especially after Marc's final rejection. "I might check out Julian over the next few weeks and see if I like it. I can settle anywhere. And won't you need secretarial help again in the spring?"

She kept in touch with only one of her foster parents, but they weren't close. She had two friends from the building department and one longtime friend from high school. They all had busy lives and wouldn't miss her as much as she'd miss them. Maybe she could start over in Julian. Find a niche for herself and her baby.

She'd long been used to knowing she was alone in the world. Having a job to look forward to in the spring would help pass the long winter months.

Jeff smiled. "You thinking about coming back when we start up again?"

"Maybe."

"And the baby?"

She looked around the office. "I think a playpen would fit in here by my desk. How long will you take to finish the project?"

"End of next summer should do it, if we keep on schedule and the winter doesn't last forever. Sorry, Mandy, girl, Jackson would never allow a baby on the site. It's too dangerous."

"Not in the office."

"It'll never happen, Mandy. I'd back him on that

decision. In fact, I need to know you'll be safe now, or I'll change my position on your staying.''

''I'm fine.'' Frustration was building. She wished she'd never gone on that blasted walk!

The phone rang.

Ten minutes later Mandy hung up, feeling hugely relieved.

''The doctor said it sounds like altitude sickness. I'm to take things easy and drink a lot of fluids. If anything else happens, then I'm to see a local doctor immediately. I was planning to set up an appointment anyway, so I'll do that first thing in the morning.''

''You're sure?'' Jeff asked. ''I don't want anything to happen to you.''

She nodded, warmed by his concern.

Hadn't Jackson also been concerned?

The warmth she felt around Jackson had nothing to do with *concern*.

''I was so excited to have someone competent come out, I guess I didn't think things through all the way,'' Jeff said slowly.

''Don't even start thinking that way. I'm competent and capable. I'm not sick. Today was an anomaly. I can do the work, Jeff. I've burned my bridges behind me. If you fire me, where would I go?'' She prayed this tactic might work with softhearted Jeff. It never would with hard-as-nails Jackson Witt.

''Anyway, I think Jackson overreacted,'' she said.

''Understandable.''

''Why?'' Did Jeff hold insight into his partner, something that, if shared, would enable her to better understand the man? To better deal with him? Could Jeff help her find a way to work around Jackson's antagonism and be allowed to remain?

"His wife and child were killed a few years ago. It eats at him that he wasn't there to save them. He probably feels he can at least make sure your baby is properly taken care of. And face it, Mandy, a construction site isn't the safest place in the world. I should have thought through the situation more before hiring you. But we need help as much as you need the job!"

She was stunned by the information about Jackson's family. How tragic! She tried to imagine a loss of that magnitude. Protectively, her hands covered her stomach. The worst fear of any parent was to lose a child. And he'd lost both wife and child?

"How were they killed?"

"Random shooting at an elementary school. Sara was a teacher there, and Sammy had just started kindergarten." Jeff's voice was heavy with grief.

"Oh, Lord." Mandy swallowed, unexpected compassion and sympathy for Jackson suddenly blooming. No wonder he was such a hard man—he'd have to be to survive such a devastating loss. "How awful!"

She wanted to weep—for the loss, for the man who must have been so devastated, so angry at fate to lose his family in such a senseless manner.

Jeff looked out the window, toward the skeleton of the lodge. "He's never been the same. He and Sara grew up together. Don't think he ever dated anyone else. And they doted on their little boy." Jeff shook his head sadly. "Tragic time."

He turned and looked at Mandy. "That's one reason he drives himself now—to forget, I think. If work is all-consuming, there's no time for memories."

"How long ago did it happen?" Her throat ached with unshed tears. Her heart went out to the man. His attitude could be excused, explained. Maybe he felt genuine concern for her and her pregnancy.

"Three years ago this month. It happened over in Fort Collins. That's where I had my company. Jackson was my foreman at the time. Afterward, he had us push for bigger jobs, remote sites, shorter time schedules. He became my partner. His ideas are great, and we're doing better than ever—but I miss that town. I don't reckon Jackson will ever go back. He hasn't seen his folks since the funeral. Or Sara's parents. We all lived in Fort Collins."

"I am so sorry," Mandy said. "What happened to the gunman?"

"He turned the gun on himself before the cops could stop him. Which makes it even harder, I think—no one around to blame. Come on, I'll walk you back to your trailer. You feeling up to it?"

"Yes."

But there was something she needed to get straight.

"But this fainting doesn't matter to my position here. I'm not traipsing around the construction site, so I'm not in danger. Please, talk to Jackson. I'll promise to do whatever you ask."

Jeff studied her for a moment, then nodded. "We'll see what he says come Friday. We're partners, Mandy. And I set a lot of store by his thinking. If we can't bring him around by Friday, then I think I'll have to go along with his decision."

She nodded, her optimism slipping. She had hoped to count on Jeff to argue on her behalf. "I understand." And she did. If the shoe had been on the other foot, would she want an employee who proved to be a liability?

"If you want to go for a walk tomorrow, tell me. I'll go with you," Jeff said as he stopped by her door.

"Thanks. I appreciate that."

"But just a gentle ramble, no trying out for the Olympics."

Mandy laughed. "I wasn't!"

He nodded and gave her a friendly pat on the shoulder. Mandy let herself out of the office, relieved that her doctor had not seemed concerned. But fainting wasn't something she wanted to repeat.

Was there a certain wisdom in Jackson's wanting her to leave?

After a hot shower and a quick meal, Mandy sat on the sofa in her living area for a long time, her mind wandering to the revelations Jeff had made, trying to assimilate the horror of the tragedy with Jackson and his family. No wonder the man was as hard as nails, she thought again. He'd have to be to survive such a loss.

It gave her a different view of her boss, maybe one she could figure out how to tap into. She not only had to prove she would be a valuable member of the team, but also that she was in no danger. Today's fainting spell had not helped. Maybe she should have him talk directly to her doctor. Would that reassure him?

Wasn't anything ever easy? she wondered with a sigh as she rose to wash her plate and utensils. It sure hadn't been so far.

The primrose-yellow dress Mandy donned the next morning was soft and feminine. She stared at herself in the mirror, suddenly struck by her image. Maybe she was her own worst enemy. No wonder Jackson doubted her abilities, her suitability at the construction site and her safety. She looked as if she were heading out for a tea party or something. Her own style in clothes was working against her.

Quickly she changed into a dark, hunter-green dress that seemed more businesslike, and tied her hair back, trying to look as competent as she could. There was only so much she could do with her hair. She frowned at her reflection, deciding she still looked too soft for a construction site.

She needed to go into town and get some jeans and flannel shirts. Her own jeans were in storage in Denver. Not that they'd fit, anyway, these days. Maybe she'd even get some boots. If she dressed like everyone else on the site, then maybe Jackson wouldn't even notice she was different.

Saturday she'd make the trip to Julian to see about expanding her wardrobe. Until then, she had only her skill and experience on the job going for her. It would have to hold her.

Neither Jackson nor Jeff were in the office when Mandy entered. She gave a sigh of relief. She had plenty to do. They'd undoubtedly have more tasks when they returned.

She liked working alone. Otherwise, she was self-conscious with Jackson staring at her, listening to her phone conversations, judging her with his critical attitude. Or distracting her by just sitting in his chair!

She had completed the calls Jackson had requested she handle, and was once again plunged into matching invoices and purchase orders. There was a discrepancy with one vendor—Andrews Tool and Die. Curious, she pulled out the folder on the company. It was thick, showing years of a business relationship with the firm.

Further research turned up other discrepancies. The

cost overruns and extra billings added up to a tidy sum over a period of several months.

Did Jeff and Jackson know this? She noted scrawled initials in the corners of the invoices. Obviously Pete had obtained approvals to pay. From whom?

When Jackson entered the office some time later, Mandy forgot about business, seeing only the man who had lost his family so tragically. She immediately wanted to extend her sympathies, but one glance at his dark expression, and she wisely kept her mouth shut.

In fact, she suddenly wondered how he'd react if he discovered Jeff had been talking about him. Today was Thursday, not an auspicious time to take a chance. She had only today and tomorrow to prove herself. Making him angry wouldn't be a smart move.

She reached for the phone when it rang. It was her doctor, checking on her again. She spoke briefly, and when she hung up, Jackson was studying her.

"My doctor. I talked with her last night and she wanted to see how I was doing today. I'm fine. She said to just take it slow adjusting to the higher altitude. Which won't be a problem. I know what to look for now, and it won't happen again!"

He gave nothing away in those dark eyes, just nodded once and returned to the site drawing he was marking.

When the phone rang again, Mandy snatched it up, grateful for the interruption. Would anything change his mind?

"Mr. Norris calling for Mr. Witt," a smooth voice on the other end said.

Mandy held up the phone. "A Mr. Norris for you." Jackson took the call.

Mandy half listened to the one-sided conversation. It was hard to get the gist from his yes and no and that-would-be-fine comments. When he hung up, he glanced over at her.

"Norris is the liaison between our firm and Windhaven's board. He'll be out next week to check on our progress."

She nodded, a small bud of hope blossoming. Was Jackson telling her because she'd be here next week and needed to know? He must be, otherwise why bother clarifying the situation?

He turned back to the clipboard he had brought into the office, and jotted some notes on a sheet of paper. Mandy watched him, wondering how he had felt when first informed of his son's death. Of the wanton killing of his wife—especially when he'd loved her since they were kids.

Mandy wondered what it would be like to be loved like that. To know someone from when she'd been little, and still have a deep relationship.

He looked up and caught her eye. "Something wrong?"

She shook her head. "Did you need me to do something special for Mr. Norris's visit?" She was glad he couldn't read minds. But she wished she could.

Jackson rocked back in his chair, balancing it on two legs as he scanned the office, apparently lost in thought. A moment later, he looked at her and brought his chair back on all four legs.

"You're an adult. Jeff convinced me last night that if you think you can be safe here, I have to grant that you can run your own life. Your work has been exemplary. But it's still early. I'm willing to give you another week's trial."

Mandy nodded, hiding the sudden glee that swept

through her. Thank goodness for Jeff. Obviously his opinion counted a lot in this partnership.

"Do you suppose you could get this place cleaned up by Monday afternoon? Norris and his team will want to go over things, and we could do it here if the place looked halfway decent."

Mandy vowed right then and there to have the office spotless by the time Monday rolled around. She had planned to make herself indispensable. Here was another way to prove it to Jackson.

Another week. How much more could she prove her worth in another week? She kept her expression pleasant, trying desperately to hide the joy that flooded her. She could do it.

And maybe get a chance to see the man smile! She blinked, wondering where that thought had come from. She didn't care if he ever smiled, as long as she stayed employed.

She resumed her review of the invoices from Andrews Tool and Die with renewed fervor. Jotting notes on a separate sheet, she realized that each invoice had billed a minor amount beyond what it should have. But when she tallied everything for the last two years, it came to a total that was staggering.

Jeff entered the office, tossing his hard hat on his desk and heading for the pot of coffee.

"That wind's cold today. Hope it's not the leading edge of a storm."

"Nothing forecast for the next week. Don't borrow trouble. I heard from Norris. He'll be here on Monday." Jackson looked up at Jeff, then nodded toward Mandy. "She said she could get the place decent by then. One of their publicists and an accountant are coming, too."

Jeff looked suspiciously at Jackson, then at Mandy.

She smiled at Jeff, wishing she could thank him for talking to Jackson after he'd seen her home last night. Later for sure, but not in front of Jackson.

"Oh, well, good. Guess she's staying, then." Jeff winked at her.

"For another week's trial," Jackson said.

He couldn't dim her delight in the extension, Mandy thought defiantly. She'd become indispensable in a week. Watch out, Jackson Witt!

The morning passed swiftly after that. Just before lunch, Mandy put down her pencil and looked at the two men. She was sure of her facts, but wasn't sure how they'd react.

"I think I've found a problem," she said slowly.

Both men looked up at her.

"It appears that one of your vendors has been siphoning off a bit more with each invoice than you have on your purchase orders."

"What vendor?" Jackson asked, glancing at Jeff.

"Andrews Tool and Die."

"Damn!" he said, rising to storm over to her desk. "Let me see that!"

"Oh, Lord!" Jeff said, sitting at his desk, his latest cup of coffee held precariously as he looked at her in dismay.

Mandy didn't know what she'd just done, but by the dark scowl on Jackson's face it had to be terrible. Was this what would get her fired?

Chapter Four

"Let me see that," Jackson repeated, holding out his hand for the folder and sheets of paper.

She held on to the folder. "I've been catching up— matching the invoices and purchase orders with the check register you send to the accountant. This batch is three months behind. I couldn't help noticing discrepancies with this account."

"It'll be taken care of," Jackson said curtly. He wiggled his fingers impatiently and Mandy reluctantly placed the folder in his hand.

He spun around and glared at Jeff. "Not a word," he warned.

Jeff shrugged and went back to his blueprint.

Mandy didn't understand. "Did you already know about it?" she asked.

Jackson dropped the file on his desk and sat down, his familiar scowl present.

"I'll take care of the matter. Why don't you take off for lunch? It's almost twelve."

Recognizing that she'd been clearly dismissed, Mandy nodded and rose. She walked carefully from the office and turned just before she closed the door behind her. Jackson was staring at the closed folder. She couldn't describe the expression on his face, but if she had to make a guess, she'd call it bleak.

"What was that all about?" she wondered aloud as she crossed the sunny clearing. Neither man had displayed the reaction she'd expected. But she wasn't sure what they had shown.

The wind was stronger than before, and carried the hint of fall in it, cool and biting. Walking briskly, she was glad to reach the shelter of her trailer. Maybe this would be all the walking she did today.

A couple of the men called a greeting. She smiled and waved. So far only Bill and Tim had introduced themselves. Though given the chance, she suspected some who wandered into the office would have, except that Jackson or Jeff had always been present.

Mandy put her feet up while she ate, relishing the brief respite in the busy day. She wondered if she'd have more energy if she upped her vitamin intake.

When the knock at the door came several moments later, she was startled. Not one of the workers, surely.

She opened it. Jackson stood at the foot of the steps. "I want to speak with you—privately," he said.

Oh Lord, was he going to fire her? Just for doing her job? Or was that the excuse he'd use?

"Come in." She stepped aside to let him in, aware again of how much he seemed to fill the small space of her living room. She wondered how he felt in his own trailer—cramped? Or was it larger than hers, offering more space?

He looked around, noticing the chair pulled up in front of the sofa, the plate with her half-eaten sandwich set to one side.

"Resting?" he asked.

"Just putting my feet up for a little while. Is this a short visit, or would you like to sit down?"

He turned and looked at her, a hint of amusement dancing in his eyes. It was as unexpected as it was intriguing. Mandy stared at him. It made him look approachable, almost human. Again she wondered what he'd look like if he ever smiled.

"You fascinate me, Mandy Parkerson," he said. "Most people in your position would be fawning over me, doing all they could to curry favor so I'll let them stay. As a welcome, your invitation lacks hospitality."

"If my work won't speak for me, fawning over you isn't going to help matters," she said shortly, flustered by the intensity of his gaze. His eyes were so dark as to be almost black. She could stare into them for hours.

"My visit won't take long, but sit back down. I don't want you interrupting your rest time." Jackson pulled one of the dining chairs from the nearby table and turned it, straddling it and resting his arms on the back. He waited until she resumed her seat on the sofa before speaking again.

"Jeff and I had a rather heated discussion after you left," he began.

"About?" She knew what about—her staying, what else?

"About the Andrews Tool and Die discrepancies you found and the need-to-know principle."

"Need-to-know principle?"

''You know, what do you need to know to do your job, and what is just...idle gossip.''

''I don't have a clue what you are talking about. I thought you came to fire me.''

''The next week's not up yet. And I'm not inclined to fire someone for doing a good job. Jeff convinced me you need to know what's going on to better do your job, and not go off half-cocked on some tangent that's already been dealt with.''

Mandy nodded, hoping her total confusion didn't show.

''Don't you want to put your feet up? You only have a few minutes left for lunch break,'' he said.

Self-consciously, she lifted her feet to the chair, glad for the full skirt that covered most of her legs. He watched her every move. It flustered her. Why had he come? What couldn't have waited until she returned to the office?

''So my need to know?'' she prompted.

''We fired Pete, right before he was arrested for embezzling funds. By the same method you uncovered today—approving padded invoices, splitting the difference with greedy clerks at the various vendors. He always did the reconciliation, so we didn't catch on right away. But we haven't advertised the fact of his arrest. I doubt any of the men here know. Jeff and I want to keep it that way.''

''He was arrested?'' It was the last thing she'd expected to hear.

Jackson nodded. ''We've kept it as quiet as possible—so as not to spook investors, and to enable law enforcement officials to find and deal with those involved at the various vendors who participated in his scheme.''

"And Andrews Tool and Die is another company involved—but one you didn't know about before," she guessed.

Jackson sighed, tightening his jaw. "Right. We never suspected it." He studied her for a moment, then continued, "Marshal Andrews is my brother-in-law."

"Uh-oh," she said softly.

Jackson gave a mirthless laugh. "Uh-oh doesn't begin to describe it. I want to handle this one differently. Jeff doesn't agree, but said he'll hold off notifying the authorities until Monday."

Mandy nodded. "I won't tell a soul."

"Discreet as well as competent," he murmured. He hesitated a moment, then added, "You could use this as a bargaining tool."

"For what?" she asked.

"For keeping your job. Your silence in exchange for continued employment."

Mandy's temper flared up. Honestly, the man was enough to drive her crazy! She didn't remember getting so angry so often in her entire life before this week. Down came her feet, and she surged up from the sofa. "That's despicable. I would never do such a thing! How dare you even suggest it!"

Standing, she was taller than Jackson. He gazed up at her, almost mesmerized by her appearance. Color stained her cheeks, the rosy hue deepening the blue of her eyes, which flashed with fire and anger. Even tied back as it was, her hair seemed to shimmer around her like a glowing halo trembling with indignant rage.

Her lips were tight with disapproval. But Jackson knew what they looked like softened, smiling. For a moment he was struck with wondering what they'd feel like. Warm and supple? Sweet and feminine?

He scowled and rose to his own feet, putting distance between them. He had no business thinking about kissing Mandy Parkerson! He'd sworn off even the thought of getting interested in another woman after Sara died. Even thinking about kissing someone else seemed a betrayal of his love for his wife.

But it had been three long years, and his body was betraying him with its reaction to this petite, feminine fireball.

"I said that you could have used this, not that you would. I don't want this to get out. Jeff and I will handle it and turn it over to the proper authorities if warranted. But I want to talk to Marshal first."

The fact was he didn't want to believe his brother-in-law would stoop to crime. He hoped for some explanation. For Sara's sake, he would investigate on his own before turning any information over to the authorities.

"Fine." Mandy continued to glare at him.

"I'll be heading back to the office." He'd gotten her compliance, but at a cost. She looked mad enough to spit!

She didn't say a word.

"Take some extra time if you need it," he said, backing toward the door, unable to take his eyes from her. Could he add something to calm the tension? Or was retreat the best plan?

"I'll be there at one," she snapped.

"Good, good." Jackson opened the door and stepped outside as quickly as he could, closing it behind him. Retreat was definitely called for. He needed his own space, away from those flashing eyes, those bewitching blond curls. She could have him forgetting his own name if she half tried.

Which, in all honesty, he had to admit she never had.

Maybe she was too good to be true. She had done nothing except do the work for which she'd been hired. No tricks, no flirting, no promising anything she hadn't delivered.

Striding quickly toward the office, he changed his mind halfway there and headed for the lake. Jackson wasn't ready to return to the tasks at hand, and certainly not ready to confront Marshal Andrews with the information Mandy had turned up.

Men drifted past, nodding, calling a greeting, heading back to the job site. Jackson acknowledged the greetings disinterestedly, lost in thought as he was. He had to come to terms with his growing awareness of Mandy Parkerson before he could do anything else.

Not awareness—not on a sexual level. That was too strong. Interest? No, not that.

She was an employee only. Nothing more.

But the memory of her sparkling eyes seemed to tease him, the curiosity about how her hair would feel continued to plague him until he could hardly keep his hands to himself. And her anger only made his fascination grow stronger, as she radiated energy he longed to lock on to.

Maybe it was the glow pregnant women had.

Like she'd be a hag when she wasn't pregnant? Hardly.

He wasn't ready to deal with this. Maybe he never would be. It was time to focus on the job and keep his distance from Mandy Parkerson and the disturbing thoughts that plagued him whenever he looked at her.

On Saturday morning Mandy slept in until nine. She reveled in knowing she had two days totally to herself. Not that she planned to spend the weekend in complete relaxation. There was more to do in the office in order to have it spotless for the meeting on Monday. But she had definitely made progress. Thanks to Jackson's staying away since lunch on Thursday.

She'd been angry when she returned to the office, only to find he was busy on the site. By Friday afternoon, when he still hadn't put in an appearance in the office, she began to wonder if he were deliberately avoiding the place. But why?

She would have thought it was because of their discussion at lunch on Thursday, but Jackson definitely was not the type to let a small confrontation like that deter him from anything he wanted to do. He'd just charge onward.

After a leisurely breakfast, she headed into Julian. She had shopping to do—both for clothes and groceries. And she wanted to explore the town and see what it was like.

Wearing the bright yellow dress she'd discarded a couple of days earlier, she decided she was still determined to buy jeans and shirts. Once that was accomplished, Mandy planned to treat herself to lunch and wander around, sightseeing a little before getting her groceries. She'd brought her cooler to carry the perishables, and she planned to stock up this trip, convinced she'd stay the course.

Some time later, she stowed the many packages of new clothes in the trunk of her car and turned to survey the main street of the small mountain town. She'd been lucky to find a clothing store that had a couple of pairs of maternity jeans that fit her, with waistbands that would expand as she did. The flannel shirts felt warm and cozy. She was into comfort more and more these days.

The boots were instantly comfortable. Maybe she should have worn her new jeans and boots and carried the dress home, she mused. But it was too late now; everything was stashed in the car.

Main Street was lined with cars and trucks parked at the curb. The old buildings were mostly wood, with a brick one here and there, and a faded brown stucco building at the far end of town. The false fronts were common in towns in Colorado, but she enjoyed looking at them nonetheless.

She walked down the street, peering into wide shop windows, enjoying the different displays of books, yarn and fabrics, hardware, wood-burning stoves and colorful liquor bottles. Finally she reached the diner. Glancing in through the windows, she stopped, reconsidering. It seemed full—mostly of men. There were five at the counter, and almost every table was occupied. She recognized a couple of men from the work site. The rest were strangers. Two women were eating at one table, but there didn't appear to be a single woman on her own.

And none dressed as she was. She should have worn her new jeans.

"Coming or going?" a familiar voice asked.

Mandy spun around to see Jackson Witt standing beside her. She glanced behind him. No Jeff.

Trying to ignore the fluttering in her tummy, she smiled brightly. "I was going in to eat, but it seems crowded." She didn't want him to know she felt intimidated.

"There're a couple of tables vacant," he said, looking over her head into the diner.

"Oh." She glanced back through the window, stalling. What was he doing here? If he'd leave, she could find another place to eat where she wouldn't stick out like a sore thumb.

"Are you in town shopping?" she asked, turning back to look at him.

"I'm here to pick up a few things, order more. We have a small order ready at the hardware store. Right now I want lunch."

"Oh."

He studied her for a moment, then sighed. "Care to join me?"

Eat with Jackson Witt? Have to sit across the table from him and talk with him for up to an hour? Her heart was already beating as fast as if she'd run a race. Her stomach felt full of butterflies. Could she eat a thing with him sitting that close? What would they talk about?

He inclined his head slightly. Aware of the seconds ticking by, Mandy nodded and took a deep breath.

"That would be nice," she said politely, hunger winning the internal debate.

When they entered, the people seated near the door glanced up, but no one seemed to pay them special attention. She wound her way through the crowded area to a vacant table near the rear and sat down gratefully, looking around curiously.

The diner had linoleum flooring and chrome-edged tables and chairs. The decor seemed straight from the 1950s. The heavenly aroma that filled the air had her mouth watering even before the waitress dropped two menus on the table and placed two brimming glasses of water before them.

"I'll give you a couple of minutes," she said, and walked away.

Marc would never have eaten in a place like this, Mandy thought, picking up the menu. He was into show and flash. And being seen. This place looked as if it served good hearty food to one and all, for inexpensive prices. No linen tablecloths, no cloth napkins. But she liked it. It had charm.

Carefully keeping her gaze on her menu, Mandy desperately sought a topic of conversation she could safely discuss with Jackson. They had nothing in common. And there was a certain amount of antagonism on his part. He wanted her gone.

Maybe she could ask him about Monday's meeting or about the future plans of the resort or—

"Ready to order?" he asked.

Mandy peeped over the menu and found his dark gaze fixed on her. She swallowed hard, hoping he couldn't guess how flustered she felt.

Nodding quickly, she looked for the waitress. Jackson signaled and the woman hurried over.

Marc would be envious of Jackson's air of command. He never received such swift attention, Mandy thought, childishly pleased in a perverse way. Much as she told herself she was over the man, the lingering hurt never quite went away.

After they ordered, she took a breath and prepared to start the conversation, but Jackson startled her by asking bluntly, "Where's your baby's father?"

She blinked. She hadn't expected that. "He lives in Denver," she said.

"And?"

"And what?"

"Why is he there and you here? A falling out?"

"You could say that. He doesn't want to be a father."

Jackson looked away, a brief expression of pain crossing his face before he schooled it to impassivity.

Mandy remembered that his own son had been killed

by a crazed gunman. Obviously Jackson was still griev-
ing. He was a father who had wanted his child. Why
couldn't her baby's father want it?

"Not all men want babies, I guess," she said.

"Then he's a fool. Being a father is the most incredible experience in the world."

"I'm sorry for the loss of your son and your wife."
There, she'd said it. She'd wanted to ever since Jeff had
mentioned it.

Jackson narrowed his eyes as he looked back at her.
"Jeff told you?"

She nodded. "I can't even imagine how awful it must
have been."

"Still is," he said shortly. "It's not something I talk
about. And Jeff has no business gossiping about me
behind my back."

"It wasn't gossip. I think he was trying to let me
know why you reacted so strongly when I fainted the
other day." She turned her water glass, watching the
ice bob gently on the surface. "I've heard it's the worst
thing, a parent losing a child. I can't imagine losing my
baby. Or giving it up." She said the words so softly she
didn't think he'd hear.

But he had.

"Did the father want you to give it up?"

"No. Actually, he wanted me to have an abortion. I
refused, and that was the end of his involvement in my
life. A child didn't fit in with his image of the perfect
life. I didn't, either." Not in the perfect, shallow exis-
tence Marc enjoyed.

"Are you thinking of giving the baby up for adoption?"

"No! I would never do such a thing." Mandy looked

directly into his eyes. "I already love this baby. I'll do anything to keep it."

"Some people, especially single women, give their kids up for adoption. It's not necessarily a bad thing."

"Well, I'm not some people. I can afford to take care of a child and I will, no matter how tough the going gets. Businesses always need good secretaries, and I am good."

"Modest, too."

She grinned. "If you've got it, flaunt it!"

"Planning to return to Denver?"

Mandy thought about it a moment. "Probably not. I have nothing to tie me there. I can really go anywhere. I might look for an apartment or small house to rent here in Julian." She looked at him. "Then I'd be handy in the spring when construction starts up again."

Jackson looked startled. "You haven't even worked through next week and you're planning to be back next spring? It'll never happen."

"We'll see." She wished he'd stop staring at her. She'd never be able to eat if her stomach didn't settle down. Or if she didn't stop feeling she was about to hyperventilate. His steady gaze made her very nervous, and very conscious that he was all male. For the first time in more than four months, she was aware of a man. Aware and growing interested.

That would never do. She had to remember her vow—no more involvement except on a superficial level. There was too much heartache in growing attached to people. They always left in the end.

"Maybe I'll find a job here in town. It seems like a nice place to raise a child. If I do a great job for you, you would write me a recommendation, wouldn't you?"

Jackson nodded, suddenly aware he didn't like thinking of her going elsewhere. Not that he wanted her to work at the site next spring. What would she do with the baby during the day?

Next spring...? What had happened to his thinking that she wouldn't last the week?

In only a few days, he'd grown used to her bright smile and unflagging optimism and energy. It was a refreshing change from Jeff's lackadaisical attitude. Or the doomsayers from Windhaven's accounting office. Jackson had stayed away from Mandy as much as he could the last couple of days, but it hadn't blotted her from his mind.

Even his quiet evening at the lake last night had been spoiled as he subconsciously waited for her to show up needing him for some crisis.

He didn't like where his thoughts were going. Hoping to shake things up, he leaned back in his chair and said, "No wonder you wanted to come to a construction site—plenty of men to choose from to take care of you and that baby."

He could have predicted her reaction. Heck, he had counted on it. Raging color flooded her cheeks, and her blue eyes deepened and flashed fire. He could swear her hair almost stood on end.

He had to give her credit, however. She didn't cause a scene, didn't dump ice water in his lap or storm out of the diner. She leaned forward, her teeth gritted.

"That's the most asinine thing I've heard in ages. You are one dumb chauvinistic male if you think women want a man in their life to take care of them. This is the twenty-first century, and I can take care of myself!"

"So you don't want a man?"

"No!"

He tilted his head slightly. She appeared to be telling the truth. But a woman alone with a baby? It had been hard enough when he and Sara shared duties with Sammy. How did single parents manage?

"Still pining for the baby's father?"

Mandy drew herself up in the chair and glared at him. "Not that it is any of your business, but no. Once he showed his true colors, I knew he was not the man for me. Had never been, in fact, but I had been blinded by his apparent interest and flattered by his attention. Heady stuff to someone who had never had it."

"Never had what?"

She glanced away, looked at her glass, finally darted a quick look at Jackson. "Love," she mumbled.

"First boyfriend?" He found that hard to believe. With that cascading blond hair, those bright eyes and her frequent smile, she probably stepped on men's hearts like some women climbed stairs.

"This is embarrassing. I don't want to discuss it."

"It isn't a discussion. Just answer the question."

"Marc was not my first boyfriend, but he was the first one I thought might stick around."

"So your mama didn't warn you about men who liked to, er, play the field?"

"My mother abandoned me when I was five. I never saw her again. My dad split before I was born."

Jackson stared at her, dumbfounded. The color in her cheeks was fading. Her eyes looked everywhere but at him.

She had been abandoned as a child? How could any parent abandon his or her own child?

The old familiar ache began. He'd give his right arm to have another minute with Sammy. Or Sara. He had spent as much time with them as he'd been able, and it hadn't been enough. How could someone just throw that away?

"What happened with your mother?" he asked, unable to imagine anyone giving up a child.

"I have no idea. I said I never saw her again. She dumped me at social services one day, told them she couldn't afford to feed me, and left before they could stop her."

"And she never contacted you again?"

Mandy shook her head. "I went into foster care. Lived with a couple of nice families—but it's not the same as blood kin."

"People don't have to be blood related to be a family," he said.

She shrugged. "It seemed like that to me growing up."

He was silent, trying to come to terms with her revelation. If he'd been abandoned by his parents, would he have such a sunny disposition? Hell, he'd been raised by doting parents and didn't have a sunny disposition.

The waitress wove her way among the tables, balancing their plates on her arms. She set them down, made sure they had everything they wanted, and sashayed away.

Jackson didn't notice. He was still trying to figure out a way to respond to Mandy's revelation. Had she tried to find her parents? She must have been an adorable little girl, since she was pretty enough to penetrate his own hard shell. How could—

"Do you come here every Saturday?" she asked brightly, obviously changing the subject.

He didn't want to change it; he wanted to know more.

But he followed her direction. It wasn't the end of their discussion, however. She just didn't know it yet.

"Every once in a while I go to Durango or up to Grand Junction. Depends if I can combine business with weekend travel. But usually Julian is as good as it gets. The food here isn't bad."

"No, it's delicious. I wasn't sure if it was just because I hadn't fixed it."

Silence stretched out between Mandy and Jackson. The soft murmur of the other diners provided background noise. Jackson didn't feel the need to say much. He'd already put his foot into it a couple of times. No sense in making matters worse.

But he didn't like the silence.

"Have you seen the town?" he asked at last.

"I was in the grocery store last Tuesday, and plan to go there after lunch to stock up for the week. And today I bought some more clothes—warmer things for the fall. I thought I'd walk around before I leave. Some of the houses on the side streets look intriguing."

"They were probably built during the gold boom, which didn't last long here. Cripple Creek drew the miners. But Victorian architecture is enduring."

"And pretty. I'm glad so many owners have been able to maintain the homes."

You couldn't get much more superficial than that, Jackson thought cynically. Maybe he should introduce the weather as the next topic.

When they finished, Mandy brought out her wallet and carefully counted out several dollars. She dropped some beside her place and held out the rest.

"Dutch, of course," she said firmly.

"We could talk about work for a minute or two and write it off," he suggested whimsically. He wouldn't pad an expense account, but she needn't know that if it would save face. It didn't set right, her paying for her lunch. He suspected every bit she saved now would help when the baby came.

Not that her preparation—or lack—was any of his business.

"I'll pay my own way," she said firmly.

The lunch crowd had thinned. They quickly paid and walked out into the afternoon sunshine.

"It's so nice in the sun, but actually quite cool in the shade," she said, tilting her face to the sunshine.

Jackson felt a kick in his gut. He wanted to kiss her, see if the sun-warmed skin tasted as sweet and warm as it looked.

"Oh!" Her eyes flew open and her hand went to her stomach. "Goodness, what a kick. Is he doing somersaults?" She looked at Jackson shyly. "Would you like to feel?" she asked hesitantly.

No! The memories of Sammy were too poignant. How often had he and Sara marveled over the feel of that little person inside her? How often had they shared the intimacies of the baby they'd created growing in his mother?

Mandy didn't wait for an answer, but took Jackson's hand and placed it on the small mound of her stomach. Jackson felt it, definitely a firm kick. Or elbow.

Memories flooded back. The aching pain threatened to overwhelm him. Before he could pull away, however, Mandy smiled up to him, pure happiness shining in her eyes.

"I've never been able to share that with anyone before. Isn't it great?"

He left his hand in place, sharing the wondrous miracle of life for as long as he could bear it. Time and place blurred. He looked at Mandy, and saw Sara. But not the strong image he was used to. She seemed fuzzy, and Mandy came into sharp focus.

Leaning over, he brushed back the soft curls, tucking them behind her ear, relishing the satiny feel of the tresses he'd so longed to touch.

"Cherish your baby, Mandy. Hold on to every precious moment."

Without another word, Jackson turned and strode off, the anguish of his loss threatening to overwhelm him.

Chapter Five

Mandy stared after the man, stunned by his gentle touch. She raised her hand to her cheek, still feeling the warmth of his fingertips where he'd brushed back her hair. Still feeling the thrill of his palm against her belly, where her baby continued to do the cancan.

She wasn't touched often, and usually in the most impersonal manner—a stranger brushing against her in a crowded street, or a friendly handshake when meeting someone. But this…it was outside her realm. Her skin felt sensitized and exceptionally responsive. Her nerve endings tingled and a vague yearning for something beyond her experience rose.

Jackson Witt was a puzzling man. Harsh and abrupt, opinionated and decisive, yet obviously capable of gentleness and perception.

Cherish your baby, Mandy. Hold on to every precious moment. The words echoed in her mind. She felt a sharp ache at his loss. How did he make it through each day, knowing his own baby was dead, their precious moments together gone forever?

She should cut him some slack. Had he changed a lot when he lost so much? What would it take to ease some of that pain?

He seemed to be a man who had cared deeply, unlike Marc, who was content to live in the moment—as long as the moment centered around him. How could she have not seen that at the time?

She was on her guard now. Not trusting her own judgment, not certain she could ever trust it, she vowed to stay away from entangling relationships, no matter how tantalizing it might be to fantasize about a man adoring her, caring for her, sharing her life.

She and her baby would be enough.

With that thought firmly locked in place, she turned in the opposite direction and started out to explore Julian.

By midafternoon, she'd tired of wandering through the quaint mountain town. She wanted to buy her groceries and get back before dark. She might take a short stroll to the lake's edge before dinner, if she had the time and inclination, but she really had had enough walking for now.

Mandy pulled into the parking slot next to her temporary home some time later. Jeff stuck his head out of a window in his trailer as she climbed from the car.

"I'll be right there to help you carry things inside," he called.

"I can manage," she said with a wave.

But he obviously didn't listen well. In two minutes he was pushing open her door, a sack of groceries in each arm.

"You shouldn't be carrying all these heavy bags. Tell the bag boy to put fewer items in each one. Makes for more bags, but if I'm not around, you won't have to strain to lift them."

Mandy hid a smile and nodded gravely. The bags weren't that heavy. She knew her limitations and wouldn't exceed them.

"Want to go for a walk later on?" Jeff asked, when all the food had been put away, and the bags of new clothes placed on her bed.

"I think I've had enough walking today, I wandered all over Julian."

"How about tomorrow, then?" he said.

"Maybe in the afternoon. I want to finish up in the office in preparation for Monday's meeting first. Shall we make it a picnic? We could walk along the lake for a while until we find a sunny place to eat."

As long as the weather held, Mandy thought she should take advantage of the location and explore all she could. She loved the quiet of the woods when the heavy equipment wasn't operating. The pristine beauty of the lake soothed her whenever she gazed at it.

"That sounds fine, Mandy girl. I'll be here around noon."

"What time will the Windhaven people arrive on Monday, do you know?"

"Not until afternoon, I expect. They usually fly into Grand Junction, drive to Julian and then out here. I bet they'll eat lunch in Julian. That's what they did last visit."

"That gives us more time to get ready, though I don't think we'll need it. I thought they'd be here first thing," Mandy said as she finished putting up the last of the canned goods.

''Naw, Paul Norris likes his comforts. Once we have a few rooms completed in the resort, I'm sure he'll stay here. But until then, he spends as little time here as he can. Julian isn't up to his standards, but it beats roughing it in a trailer.''

Mandy was reminded of Marc and his love for expensive restaurants and first-class accommodations. Paul Norris sounded like that. Why did men like that get into jobs where they had to rough it?

Her thoughts veered toward Jackson. He didn't seem to mind roughing it. He fit right in with the rough-and-tumble site, the rugged, rustic camp. A man's man.

Yet he'd proved today he had a tender side, as well.

Her heart skipped a beat. She had to stop thinking about him, about their lunch and the sweet way he'd brushed back her hair before he'd left so abruptly.

''Do they come often?'' she asked, trying to focus on anything but Jackson Witt.

''Every couple of months, so far. I expect this to be the last visit until we start up again in the spring. What can I bring for the picnic?'' Jeff asked.

''Not a thing. I'll pack some sandwiches and drinks. There's a big blanket in the closet that will be perfect. You can carry everything.''

''Done. See you then.'' Jeff patted her on the shoulder as he left.

Mandy felt a warmth toward the man, unlike the fluttering feelings she experienced around Jackson. If she was up to another risk, she might wish to get to know Jeff better. Was he lonely, living so far from his home, knowing he probably wouldn't go back to Fort Collins anytime soon? At least not as long as he followed his footloose partner.

Turning, Mandy wandered back into her postage-stamp-size kitchen. Maybe she'd bake something for their picnic. It would give her a chance to be creative. And hopefully take her mind off Jackson Witt. The incident at lunch replayed over and over in her mind. She needed to do something to dislodge that!

Early Sunday morning, Mandy headed for the office to prepare for Monday's meeting. She dusted all the desks and chairs and bookcases, straightening the piles of paper on the partners' desks. Looking around the office some time later, she smiled in pride. The office looked professional and a whole sight better than the first day she'd seen it.

It was a bit cramped with the makeshift conference table in the center, but with everything put away, it would do. Time to get ready for her picnic.

She donned loose denim shorts and sturdy walking shoes for her outing with Jeff. Her pink cotton top was loose, the color flattering. Her stomach still didn't stretch it to its limits. She would need maternity tops before long, but until then a slightly larger size of clothing proved sufficient.

She tied a Denver Broncos sweatshirt around her neck. They'd be home long before the late afternoon shadows cooled things down, but she wanted to be prepared just in case.

She might even go wading in the lake if it got warm enough. The air had been still that morning, and when she'd walked from the office back to her trailer, the sun had felt positively hot!

Checking the paper grocery sack that held their lunch, she waited impatiently for Jeff. She was looking forward to the outing, and to the chance to get to know the older man better.

Ten minutes past noon, Mandy began to wonder if she'd mixed up the time. Had Jeff forgotten? Had something else come up?

She could run next door and see. She was halfway to the door when the knock came. There, he'd just been delayed.

She flung it open, her smile wide and happy. "I thought—" Mandy stopped, her smile fading. Jackson stood on her step.

He looked at her, frowning. "Jeff said you needed something carried."

"Where's Jeff?"

"He took a run up to Grand Junction. Seems Paul Norris and his entourage decided to arrive today. They plan to stay the night in Julian and show up here first thing tomorrow."

"Oh, I thought they were coming after lunch."

"So did we all. Does that pose a problem?"

"No. The office is ready. Thanks for telling me about Jeff." She was disappointed. She'd been looking forward to their picnic.

"What is it you need carried?"

"What? Oh, that." She shrugged, hoping to hide her disappointment. "Jeff and I were going on a picnic. I said I'd fix the food. His contribution was to carry everything. He doesn't think I should lift anything heavier than a pencil, you know."

"A picnic?" Jackson said the words as if they were in a foreign language.

"We were going to hike along the lake, find a sunny spot and eat. You know, a picnic? Eat outside?"

"I know what a picnic is, only no one around here goes on them."

"Well, I plan to." She tilted her chin. Just because

Jeff couldn't come didn't mean she couldn't stick to her plan. The paper bag and blanket weren't all that heavy.

"I'll go with you," Jackson said.

Mandy blinked. "What?" That was the last thing she expected.

"To carry things. Unless you don't want me to."

Jackson go on a picnic with her? Just the two of them? Consternation threatened. She'd had enough trouble trying to talk to him yesterday.

Not to mention dealing with the curious sensations that swept through her whenever he was near. Such as an increased heart rate and difficulty taking a deep breath. Even thinking!

How would she manage a picnic with the man?

"That would be great." She tried to infuse some enthusiasm into her voice. "Can you spare the time?"

"I don't work 24/7. No one works on Sundays— unless we get too far behind schedule to skip a day off. And so far we're close to being on target. Besides, I could use a chance to get away. Where's the basket?"

She stepped aside to allow him to enter, gesturing to the bag and blanket on the dining table. He crossed to pick them up.

"It's heavy," he said, tucking the bag in one arm effortlessly, slinging the blanket over one shoulder.

"I didn't know what Jeff would like or how much he'd eat, so if anything, I erred on the side of a lot of food. I have three kinds of sandwiches, two kinds of chips, fruit, brownies, colas and napkins and all. Also a bottle of sparkling cider and cups. I, um, thought we could toast a productive meeting with the Windhaven people," she confessed reluctantly. He'd probably think she was nuts, but she wanted to feel part of the team, and knew Jeff would have appreciated her gesture. "We can leave that here, if you like."

"I like cider."

"Oh."

"You also said brownies? Homemade?"

"Of course. Do you like brownies?"

"I love them. I haven't had any in…" He frowned and headed for the door. "In a long time."

"Which way along the lake is best?" Mandy's hands shook a little as she locked her door. She couldn't believe she was going to have lunch a second day in a row with Jackson Witt!

Would he touch her again today? Want to feel the baby if it moved again? Brush back her hair, tangle his fingers in her curls and draw her closer for a kiss?

A kiss!

Oh Lord, she was in trouble if she let her thoughts go in that direction! Mandy shook her head, refusing to give in to fantasy. She hardly knew the man. He was her boss! Besides, she'd sworn off involvement, and a kiss would surely lead to at least thinking about involvement.

"We'll go to the right," he said, slowing his long strides to accommodate her shorter ones.

Right, in the opposite direction from where he headed after work each day. Where did he go? Was there something to the left he didn't want her to see?

Determined to enjoy herself despite the unease she felt, Mandy looked around her. The lake sparkled in the sunshine. A deep blue, it seemed to stretch on forever. The trees surrounding it were dark green, their trunks rising forty feet or higher. She heard no birds, but could hear squirrels chattering in the branches and in the dis-

tance the sound of an animal moving through the underbrush. Deer?

They walked in silence. She vowed she wouldn't be
the one to break it. She hadn't asked Jackson to accompany her, he'd volunteered. Let him be the one to start
the conversation. Besides, she hadn't a clue what to talk
about.

After a while it became harder and harder to keep
quiet. She longed to share her enjoyment of the day,
exclaim how pretty the lake looked. Share how the still-
ness fed her soul.

She darted a quick look at Jackson. His jaw was set,
his eyes narrowed against the sun's glare as he stared
straight ahead. Did he even notice where they were?
For all the attention he paid, they could be walking
through a concrete tunnel.

Mandy halted abruptly and held out her hand. "I'll
take my lunch and blanket. You can go back."

"What?" He stopped a couple of steps ahead and
turned back to look at her. "What are you talking
about? I thought we were going on a picnic."

"You look as if you're going to an execution. Picnics
are supposed to be fun. I certainly can go by myself. I
don't need you to put yourself out to accompany me!"

"I'm not putting myself out to do anything. I haven't
eaten lunch. We'll eat what you fixed."

She lowered her hand indecisively. "I know you
can't seem to manage a smile, but at least take that
scowl off or I'll think you're having a terrible time."

His features relaxed somewhat. "And that's important—what kind of time I'm having?" he asked.

She shrugged. "This is a gorgeous day, we are in a
pristine setting. Pretend you're having a good time, if
nothing else."

He glanced around at the trees, the lake, then back at her. "I'm enjoying myself." He said it with a hint of surprise.

"Oh. Well, then. Good." She smiled and started walking again, almost as surprised as he sounded. A moment later she glanced over her shoulder and found he was still standing where he'd stopped, staring at her legs!

Realizing she'd halted, he looked up and started walking again, catching up with her in three quick strides.

Mandy experienced a wave of feminine satisfaction. Often she felt ungainly as she grew larger with her baby. Jackson's obvious male appreciation of her legs had her glowing inside.

"How far do you plan to walk before having this feast?" he asked a few minutes later.

"I didn't plan on any set time. I thought when we found a nice spot, we'd just stop."

"There speaks a woman who is either not hungry or too picky for words."

She laughed. "Hungry, huh?"

"Yeah. I keep thinking about those brownies."

"Then how about over there?" She pointed to a wide, picturesque spot on the lakeshore. The slope to the lake was gradual. Pine needles cushioning the ground would make it comfortable to sit, and the dappled sunlight would keep them warm but not hot.

He spread out the blanket with little effort and sat on one side, setting the bag in the center. Mandy knelt opposite and began to pull the lunch from the bag. She spread it out and let him choose the sandwiches he wanted, the chips. Without a word, she opened the sparkling cider and filled two cups.

"Here's to coming in on schedule and under budget," she said, offering him one and raising hers slightly.

He nodded, taking his paper cup and brushing the edge against hers. Then he drained it.

They ate in companionable silence. Jackson raised one knee, resting his arm on it while he used the other hand to eat with. His gaze was on the lake, but from the expression on his face, Mandy had a feeling he wasn't enjoying the view.

She was having a great time. She loved listening to the soft lapping of the water and the sounds of nature surrounding them. In the distance she could again hear movement in the underbrush. A hawk lazily circled in the sky. Even the quiet man beside her added to her enjoyment. Would she ever feel comfortable around him? Not be so aware of his every move, his every expression? Despite his lack of enthusiasm, the day was perfect.

She felt more satisfaction when Jackson took a second sandwich.

"It's a nice lunch, Mandy. Thanks," he said, catching her gaze on him.

"Thank you for carrying it here. So Jeff went to Grand Junction. When did Mr. Norris call?"

"Yesterday. The message was on the answering machine when I went into the office after I returned from Julian. Jeff volunteered to go pick them up."

"Oh." He'd had time last night or even this morning before he'd left to let her know of the change in plans. Why hadn't he?

She glanced at Jackson. Had Jeff hoped she'd accept him as a substitute, and lunch together would help them hammer out their differences so they'd work in better harmony? She should have told Jeff they'd had lunch together yesterday. Their relationship was just fine— tenuous, but Jackson hadn't fired her yet.

"Do you go on a lot of picnics?" Jackson asked.

"No, this is the first in years. It's so beautiful here. Peaceful. I wonder how much it'll change when the resort is fully operational."

"A lot, I'd guess. But that's progress. Come stay sometime when it's open, and compare."

"At the rates they'll probably charge, it would be a short stay!"

"Umm." He reached for a brownie.

Mandy watched as he savored the chocolate dessert. With a quick glance at her, he took a second one. Then he grew solemn again and stared back at the lake— almost as if he were brooding.

"Is there something wrong?" she asked a few moments later.

He flicked her a glance. "No."

"You don't seem to be exactly enjoying yourself."

"I'm fine."

She watched him for a couple of moments. "Problems on the site?"

"No."

"Worried about Windhaven's inspection?"

"No. Leave it, Mandy."

She took a breath, casting around for something else to say.

"Andrews Tool and Die," she exclaimed. "Did you talk to them?"

He nodded once, abruptly.

"And?"

"And what do you want to know? They were siphoning off funds. We knew that. Any legitimate reasons? No.''

''So you'll turn it over to the authorities?''

''Already did, yesterday morning.''

''I'm sorry.''

He shrugged. After another moment of silence, he spoke. ''The hell of it was, he thought I'd let it go.''

She was startled. ''Because of the family ties?''

''Yeah. Because I was married to his sister, he thought I would turn a blind eye to criminal activities.''

''He doesn't know you very well, does he?''

Jackson looked at her. ''What?''

''Dishonesty isn't your suit.''

Jackson stared at her for a long moment, his dark eyes steady. Then he said, ''Family loyalty, guilt, whatever—he thought I'd cover for him.''

''Where was his family loyalty?'' she asked gently. ''I don't have family, but even I know you don't cheat your family or friends.''

Jackson held her gaze for a long moment. ''Good point. He threatened to drag me down with him. He plans to say I was in on it from the beginning.''

''As if anyone would believe him. From the few days I've been here, and from the vendors and officials I've spoken with, I know your reputation is sterling. A desperate man—one in the wrong—can sling whatever bull he wants, but it doesn't mean it'll stick.''

Jackson laughed.

Mandy was dumbstruck. His entire demeanor changed with the laughter. Her heart skipped a beat. He was downright make-your-heart-stop gorgeous. He should smile all the time.

Or maybe not, if he wanted anyone to get anything done. Not that the men would notice, but any woman who saw him would stop everything to soak up that male beauty.

"You're priceless, Mandy Parkerson. Sweet and pretty as a summer's day, but such language! It doesn't fit the image."

Sweet and pretty? He thought she was pretty? She swallowed, suddenly feeling shy. Casting around for something to do, she began to gather up the remnants of the picnic, uncertain whether to be flattered at the description or annoyed that he was laughing at her.

"When plain speaking is needed, I can deliver," she said.

Jackson's eyes danced in amusement but he wisely refrained from saying another word.

After she had the things packed away in the bag, he stretched out on the blanket and closed his eyes. Mandy gazed dreamily at the water, thinking about his suggestion that she visit after the resort was finished. Could she and her baby come back sometime? When the child was old enough to understand, she could explain how she'd worked on the construction site, could compare the way it would be then with the way it was today. Maybe even come to this very spot with her son or daughter.

And remember her picnic with Jackson. And his compliment. She would cherish it all the more, knowing he normally didn't say such things—especially to her. Was this a temporary truce brought on by good weather and brownies?

She glanced at him. He appeared to be asleep. She debated lying down, but eating had refreshed her. After sitting for so long, she found that any tiredness from the walk and morning work had fled. The sun had moved, their filtered shade becoming intense sunshine.

She'd tossed her sweatshirt to one side when they began to eat. Now she was growing warmer in just her T-shirt.

The lake beckoned.

She rose and walked to the edge, reaching over to feel the water. Where it was so shallow, it felt warm. Giving in to impulse, she toed off her shoes and pulled off her socks. Stepping gingerly into the water, she wiggled her toes. The pine needles that lined the bottom of the lake disintegrated and drifted around her feet like tiny confetti. Slowly she walked along, watching where she was going, looking for rocks or debris.

Wading a little deeper, she felt the water grow cooler the farther she went. Soon she was up to her knees. She stirred up the muck as she walked, making the water cloudy. It was still crystal clear ahead of her, and she saw a small school of minnows dart one way, then another.

Suddenly she stepped on a rock covered in slime and her foot slipped. Wildly trying to catch her balance, she fell to her hands and knees with a splash that wet the front of her shorts and shirt.

"What the hell are you doing?" Jackson roared from behind her.

Mandy struggled to get to her feet, her hands and knees stinging. She must have scraped them when she cushioned her fall. But the bottom was slippery and she couldn't get her footing.

Splashing behind her alerted her to Jackson's arrival. His strong hands came under her arms and he effortlessly pulled her up, setting her carefully on her feet and then wrapping his arms around her. His arms were like bands of steel, steady and strong. He had her pressed against his hard chest.

The warmth felt good against her damp shirt. She looked up into angry eyes.

"You don't have the sense God gave a mongoose. What do you think you're doing?" he almost yelled.

"Wading. It's hot. I didn't know it would be so slippery." She clung to him, feeling shaken from her fall. Her wet hands left prints on his shirt. He didn't move his arm, and she was grateful for the support. Her heart raced—a remnant of her fall, or from Jackson's proximity?

"I think I can make it to shore," she said, gaining her balance. One step, and her foot slipped again. She clutched his arm.

With a short expletive, he swung her into his arms and took three strides, depositing her on the dry shore, water streaming from his shoes and the bottom of his jeans.

"You need a keeper. Stay out of the water! Honestly, no wonder your boyfriend left, you are so much trouble! You needlessly put yourself and that baby at risk. You come to a construction site miles from anywhere—totally inappropriate for a woman, especially a pregnant woman. And then you don't even take care of yourself! What if you'd fallen into a sinkhole? Or hit your head on a rock? You could have drowned!"

He stood, hands on hips, glaring at her as he yelled.

Mandy met his gaze unflinchingly. He was right—to a degree—but still overreacting. And his comment about Marc hurt. He hadn't left because of anything she'd done—except get pregnant.

"I'm fine," she said stiffly. No one had asked Jackson to rescue her. She could have managed.

As if she hadn't spoken, he continued, raking his fingers through his hair. "This isn't going to work. I can't worry about a construction site, about the investigation into Pete's embezzlement, and watch over you at the same time!''

''No one asked you to watch over me. Don't worry about me. I've made it this far on my own, and I'll make it the rest of my days on my own.''

''And at the rate you're going, the rest of your days will number two! You need to leave, Mandy, before something serious happens.''

''Don't you dare start that again, Jackson Witt. I'm not going anywhere! I'm perfectly okay here. You don't have to nursemaid me, or worry. I don't need you or anyone else to act as guardian angel. I'm not your responsibility.''

He turned and looked out across the lake, his hands dropping to his sides, clenching into fists. ''Given my track record, maybe that's a damned good thing.''

Without another word, he started walking back to camp.

Mandy let him go, watching until he disappeared around the bend. Then she remembered what Jeff had said—that Jackson felt responsible about not being able to keep his wife and son safe. Was he thinking about them with that last comment?

She walked to her shoes and socks, wringing out as much water from her T-shirt as she could. She scooped up the shoes and took them to the blanket. Sitting, she dried off her feet and legs and put them on. She pulled on the sweatshirt. It was warm from the sun and felt good over her damp clothes.

She'd enjoyed the afternoon—most of it. Folding the blanket, she picked up the picnic bag and rose, wishing she'd handled things differently. Wishing their time together hadn't ended so ignominiously.

Maybe she *had* been a little foolhardy in going wading without knowing more about the situation. And she hadn't needed to go so far out into the water. The ankle-deep shallows had no slippery rocks.

But she was not Jackson's responsibility and he had no call to feel she was. Or make a comment about her personal life. Fat lot he knew. Marc had cut out because of the baby. Though even before that, she'd had uneasy moments. They had not been seeing eye to eye on a few other things. His values were not hers. He was into conspicuous consumption, wearing expensive clothing, taking her to expensive restaurants and making sure they had the best table, and constantly bragging on how much he was making in the stock market. Mandy would have been equally satisfied with walks along Sixteenth Avenue, or taking in a movie, or even a quiet night at home.

Rounding the bend, she saw Jackson walking back toward her. Without a word, he reached for the bag and blanket. She relinquished them and took a deep breath.

"I'm sorry for causing you to be upset," she said. "I won't go wading in the future. At least not until after the baby comes. I am taking care of myself. I won't do anything to harm my baby."

He nodded, turning to start back to camp.

"So I stay?" she asked, falling into step with him. She needed that point cleared up.

"At least through Norris's visit."

"At least until we close up for winter," she countered.

They walked in awkward silence. Mandy longed for the anticipation she'd felt on the outward journey, the joy in the day—not this uneasy tension that shimmered between them.

No tender brushing back her hair today. No sharing in the baby's movements.

She felt disappointed, discouraged and depressed when she reached her trailer.

He handed her the bag and blanket. "Get into some dry clothes."

She nodded, too dispirited to argue. Did he think she was going to sit around in wet, cold clothes? He could give her a little credit.

"In the future, stay out of trouble. I'm going to take you at your word, that you'll be fine. But you're on your own. Being with you is too much a threat to my sanity."

She watched him walk away again, feeling as low as she had when Marc had told her he wanted nothing to do with the baby.

How could one reckless act ruin her entire day?

And how could she compare Jackson's leaving with Marc's?

Chapter Six

Jackson entered the office and shut the door behind him. For a moment, he stood still, letting his eyes get used to the dimmer light. His emotions were roiling. Dammit, he should have told Jeff to get one of the other men to carry Mandy's things. Or demanded more of an explanation of what things Jeff had been talking about.

And once he'd found out about the picnic, he should have turned and left.

A setup. Jackson knew one when he saw it. His partner was doing all he could to convince him Mandy Parkerson should remain. But Jackson didn't know how much longer he could put up with the turmoil she caused.

He'd been fine these last couple of years. Going through the motions of work, finding solace in the twilight hours before dinner. The searing pain of losing

Sara and Sammy had eased. And he'd been able to get through each day.

He had definitely not been disturbed by flashes of a beguiling smile, or blond hair that had him itching to find out if those curls would wrap themselves around a man's fingers and never let go.

He walked to his desk, sat down and surveyed the office with a scowl. Dammit, she was good at her job. It would be so much easier if she fit his first expectation—an airhead intent on flirting with every man on the project.

Instead, she'd knuckled down and pushed to get the office organized. Had ignored the men on the project. And raised havoc in his own mind.

The office was the cleanest he'd ever seen it. She'd done a great job preparing for the meeting. Why couldn't she just focus on that—do her work, rest in her trailer? Stay out of his way!

Why go to lunch in Julian in a dress that looked like soft sunshine? Why talk about a little backwater town with wonder and delight in her voice? Or share her story of a childhood that sounded bleak and loveless?

So different from his.

Yet they'd both ended up in the same place, running from the blows life had dealt.

It should establish a bond between them. But he didn't want any bond. Any connection. His life was going the way he wanted—no complications, no demands, no responsibilities for another person, just the work at hand.

He'd already failed once—failed to keep his wife and child safe. Failed to keep his own heart from shattering. He wasn't strong enough to try again.

He reached for the thick folder that had all the reports

for Norris. Work had gotten him through Sara's and Sammy's deaths. Work would get him through this. Only two months remained until he and Jeff planned to shut down for the winter. He could last two months by focusing strictly on work. Ignore the soft feminine body that was so enticing when Mandy walked beside him. Ignore the fantastic legs that had almost had him drooling earlier in the day. Forget his fascination with her hair.

Ignore, refute, deny the sexual awakening he felt when she was near, when he smelled her sweet scent, when she smiled at him and all the joy of the day shone in her eyes.

Two months. He could hold out for two months.

On Monday morning Mandy dressed in her new jeans and boots. A loose T-shirt beneath her flannel shirt gave her the option of removing the flannel shirt later if she got too warm. She did her best with her hair, taming it slightly beneath a wide band. Studying herself in the mirror, she hoped she looked competent and rugged— totally suitable to be secretary on a remote construction site.

She couldn't deal with Mr. Norris siding with Jackson in wanting her to go. For a moment, she considered not showing up. But that wouldn't be professional. She would not let Jeff down like that. She was one of the team, and now she looked the part.

She was at her desk by eight.

Jackson didn't show up until the entourage from Windhaven arrived. He'd been over every inch of the construction area to make sure it would show well if Norris wanted a tour.

Jeff entered first, congenially waving the others into the office.

A tall, thin man with gray hair entered next. His dark suit looked out of place to Mandy after a week of seeing jeans and hard hats. His shirt was snowy white, his tie a dark red.

Following him was a younger man carrying a brief-case in one hand and laptop computer bag in the other. He, too, sported a dark suit and power tie.

The third member of the Windhaven group was a woman. Tall and slender with short, dark hair, she was dressed in a charcoal-gray suit, the skirt of which barely came to midthigh, showing off spectacular legs. The high heel shoes she wore emphasized the long length of those legs. No blouse, just a hint of lace at the deep V of the jacket. It was the perfect look for a woman on the move up. Or on the prowl, Mandy thought with a surprising spurt of cattiness. Jackson had best watch out for *her* distracting the men!

The woman's makeup was flawless, her composure confident. Her gaze darted everywhere, taking in everything. She spotted Mandy and a finely plucked eyebrow rose.

Jackson brought up the rear and closed the door.

Introductions were quickly made. Deirdre Evans represented the PR department of Windhaven. She gave Mandy a quick, insincere smile.

Paul Norris showed no surprise at meeting Mandy. Jeff must have filled him in on her status on the ride from Grand Junction.

George Peters, the accountant, scarcely acknowledged her presence. He was too busy setting up his laptop.

"I didn't realize you had a woman secretary," Deirdre said to Jackson when everyone sat around the long, makeshift conference table Mandy had prepared for the meeting. Deirdre drew her own chair slightly closer to Jackson than Mandy had placed them. "That doesn't cause complications?"

Mandy remained at her desk. She was not needed for this meeting, but couldn't disappear. She had work to do. And wanted to be ready if they needed more coffee or pencils sharpened.

"She hasn't been here long," Jackson said shortly.

Mandy almost held her breath, but he didn't add that she'd be leaving soon. Or that she wreaked havoc on the site. But he said nothing further.

"It must be so interesting to work in what's traditionally a man's field," Deirdre said across the room to Mandy.

"Actually, I'm the secretary—traditionally a woman's field. I don't work on the actual construction, just in the office."

Deirdre smiled again and dismissed her.

Obviously seeing me as no competition, Mandy thought wryly. She couldn't blame her. Maybe today wasn't the most auspicious day to have worn her jeans. On the other hand, her loose dresses did not convey sleek sophistication. In that field, Deirdre won hands down.

Try as she might as the morning progressed, Mandy was unable to ignore the others to concentrate on her own duties. She'd find herself listening to the conversations, glancing up once in a while—usually when Jackson was speaking. Just to learn more about the project, she assured herself, gazing at his confident presentation and response to any and all questions posed.

She wasn't the only one. Deirdre virtually ignored

the others at the table, focusing exclusively on Jackson. Of course, she already knew her Windhaven colleagues. Was this her first time meeting Jackson, or did she always behave that way?

If she thought she could get away with it, she'd probably drape herself over his arm and latch on, Mandy thought as she divided her attention between Jackson and Deirdre, growing frustrated.

She was not jealous, she told herself, just watching out for her boss. Any competent secretary would do so.

As lunchtime drew near, Paul Norris said he wanted to return to Julian to eat. Mandy noticed that neither Jeff nor Jackson voiced any opposition. Were they glad for the break? Or was the meeting concluding?

"I'll ride with Jackson," Deirdre said, smiling at him provocatively. "He can tell me more about the area. I need more information to fully exploit the potential in our marketing strategy."

Mandy had her own ideas on what Deirdre wanted to fully exploit.

From the look on Jackson's face, Mandy suspected the last thing he wanted was to be alone with the woman for any length of time—much less the duration of the ride to Julian.

"Oh, I'm sorry. Jackson, did you forget that call that's coming in at noon? It's really important—from Jasper," Mandy interjected. He could take the lifeline or not, but she'd done her best.

He looked at her and nodded, taking a deep breath. "I had forgotten it was today. I'll have to skip lunch." He looked at Paul. "When you get back, we'll cover the site. You can see the progress and ask any other questions that arise."

Jackson stood, on the far side of his chair from Deirdre, and nodded to her. "Mandy can show you around after lunch. You shouldn't be in the actual construction zone in those shoes you're wearing."

Paul stacked his reports and left them in a pile at his place. "We'll be back around three. A brief tour will be enough. We assessed the progress when we drove in. Deirdre, you might want to get a woman's perspective of this place by talking to Mandy. Get her to show you what she likes here."

Deirdre was definitely not pleased, but she kept her composure and nodded agreeably, with only her flashing eyes indicating her annoyance. "I'm a woman, in case you forgot, Paul. But another's view would be helpful, I'm sure."

Mandy knew that had not been Deirdre's plan. Any comments she herself offered would probably be ignored. Deirdre had already made her disinterest known.

Once Jeff and the Windhaven group left, Jackson leaned against his desk, crossed his arms over his chest and looked at Mandy.

"I owe you—big-time."

"Not up to lunch with Deirdre?"

"Or the ride in. What a shark, sleek and deadly. Who the hell is Jasper?"

Mandy smiled and shrugged. "I haven't a clue. The name just popped into mind. But a good secretary knows when to throw her boss a lifeline."

He nodded. "I'll keep that in mind. Are you up to showing Deirdre around this afternoon? I probably should have asked you before volunteering your services."

"But it was do-or-die time. That's fine. We can walk to the lake. Even in those shoes she's wearing." Mandy didn't say any more about the inappropriateness of the woman's attire for reviewing a construction site.

"However," she said, "something tells me she'll want a tour by the top dog of where the lobby will be, so she can write something wonderful about the view. And where the pool will be, so she can rhapsodize about its gem of a setting and where the—"

"I get it. If she makes a fuss, Jeff gets that assignment. Jasper's going to dump something big that I need to deal with immediately." His eyes held amusement as he studied Mandy. "Pete never thought so fast on his feet."

"He had other priorities, I suspect," she said dryly.

The amusement left Jackson's face. "So he did. You look different today."

"I've tamed my hair as much as I can and I'm wearing jeans."

"Why?"

She blinked. She thought he'd appreciate her looking more like she belonged on the site.

"To blend in, so you wouldn't even notice I was here," she said slowly, wondering if she were revealing too much.

He shook his head. "Never happen." He straightened and headed for the door. "Take lunch. They'll be back far too soon for my peace of mind. I'm going out to make sure everything's ready for the great inspection."

Mandy nodded, watching him leave. Her heart skipped a beat. She'd done good, and he knew it.

And she'd continue to do good, she vowed after lunch, when she and Deirdre were making their way down to the lakeshore. She'd give the woman no excuse to complain about her to Jackson.

Deirdre looked everywhere but where she was going.

When one of the workers gave a wolf whistle, she smiled and waved, almost preening.

Mandy rolled her eyes. Not too discerning, she thought. And just the type of woman Jackson did not want on the site. Deirdre probably relished setting men on end.

"So are you pregnant or just a little pudgy?" Deirdre asked once they'd left the building behind them.

"Pregnant," Mandy replied quietly. Tact wasn't Deirdre's strong point, either.

"Poor you. Is that why you are here, in the back of beyond—because your husband works on the site?"

"No." Mandy had no intention of telling this woman anything about her life.

"Then?"

"For the money," she said, suspecting that would be an explanation Deirdre would understand. It was.

"Ah, combat pay? They would have to pay extra to entice anyone out here, I'd think. Julian is not exactly Chicago."

Mandy made no reply. Let the woman think what she would. Mandy was growing to love working here. The setting was perfect, the job interesting and never boring. But she suspected Deirdre would never see it that way.

Jeff was a great boss—gave her directions, then let her do the work without micromanagement.

Jackson…well, nothing in life was perfect.

"Is Jackson Witt married?" Deirdre asked abruptly.

"No." They reached the lake. Mandy gazed at the beauty and felt the serenity almost envelop her. She was not going to gossip about her boss.

"Living with anyone?"

"What?"

"Jackson," Deirdre said impatiently. "Is he involved with someone?"

Mandy shook her head. "Not interested, I think."

"Oh, men are always interested—with the right woman."

Mandy thought about Marc. He would be interested—more than interested—if Deirdre threw a lure out his way. For a moment Mandy wondered if she could introduce the two of them. If ever two people deserved each other, it would be Deirdre and Marc!

"Do you want to walk along the shore?" Mandy asked.

"What's there to see that we haven't already seen? Once the resort is up and running, there'll be plenty of activity, but right now it's water and trees."

"It's quieter if we walk that way. The view is different. Once we round that bend over there, we can't see or hear the construction and the lake really opens up so we can see down the full length of it."

"Why bother? A lake is a lake. I've seen enough. I'd get a better impression of things from the building. See what guests would see from the lobby, that kind of thing."

Mandy hid a smile as they turned and walked back. "Have you been doing this kind of work for long?"

"A couple of years. Windhaven is an international firm, you know. My goal is Europe. But I have to work my way up. If I do a great job with this project, I'll be in a better position to request my own assignment next time. Let's stop back in the office. Maybe Jackson is through with whatever he had to do and he can show me the building site. Better than risking you showing me, in your condition and all," Deirdre said.

As if that was the reason, Mandy thought wryly.

George, the accountant, was busily comparing reports with data on his computer when they entered. Jackson and the others were not present. Deirdre frowned. "Where's Jackson?" she asked her colleague.

"He and Jeff are showing Paul something," George said vaguely, not taking his eyes from his computer.

Deirdre gave an exclamation of frustration and reached out to snag one of the extra hard hats from a hook near the door.

"I'll find them. Thanks for showing me around," she said to Mandy. Placing the hat on her head at a cocky angle, she walked out.

"Maybe I should go with her," Mandy said aloud, wondering how far she'd get before Jackson saw her. Would he hold her responsible for turning Deirdre loose?

"She can find her way," George murmured. "Or get someone to help her. She's good at that."

Mandy went to her desk and sat. There was always plenty to do without baby-sitting visitors.

It was almost dark by the time Jackson returned to the office.

"Paul's ready to leave," he told George. From the look of frustration on his face, he'd had enough of Windhaven's inspection. He glanced at Mandy.

"Deirdre find you?" she asked.

"Jeff gave her a tour of the site. She said she has enough information to write a draft. Then she'll ask for our input. Like I know anything about publicity or marketing."

"Can I take this last batch of invoices with me?" George asked. "I didn't get through as much as I thought I would."

"Mandy can make copies for you of anything you want. We always send attachments when billing," Jackson replied.

"I know, but this would give me a head start."

"Fine. I'll tell Paul you'll be out in a few minutes." Jackson turned to leave.

Mandy joined Jackson in front of the office twenty minutes later as Jeff prepared to drive Paul, Deirdre and George to Julian. He was staying in town with the Windhaven group and would take them to Grand Junction for their flight the next morning.

"Did it go well?" she asked as the car pulled away.

"As good as it gets, I guess," Jackson replied. "At least they don't plan to return until spring, unless something major turns up."

"Like a new view from the lobby," Mandy said quietly.

Jackson sighed and nodded. "God, I'm beat. Dealing with them is worse than working in the pouring rain. I'm heading for home."

Mandy watched him walk away, then turned to close the office.

Bill and Moose waved. Tommy called a greeting as she headed for her own trailer.

She was gradually getting to know the men. But, ever conscious of Jackson's views, she made no attempt to develop a friendship with anyone.

She passed Jackson's trailer on the way to hers. Would he take his walk along the lake this late? It was almost dark. Before long he wouldn't be able to see much without a flashlight.

Though with the tough day behind him, he might long for the solitude of the lakeshore.

As she let herself into her trailer, she had an idea. She could take him some more of the brownies she'd made on Saturday. If not, she'd end up eating them all, and she didn't need the extra pounds—especially after Deirdre's comment.

Mandy went directly to the kitchen to fill a small plate with brownies. Covering them with plastic wrap, she hesitated. He wouldn't see this as fawning, would he?

Before she could let doubt rule, she headed out. If he had left for his walk, she could always bring the brownies back home, or leave them on his steps.

Jackson opened the door at her hesitant knock.

"I thought you might like something special after the all-day meeting. There's nothing like chocolate to perk someone up!" she said, offering the plate.

He looked at the plate and then at Mandy. After a moment, he stood aside and opened the door wider. "Come in."

The second Mandy stepped inside, she saw that his trailer was newer, bigger and better furnished than hers. Which made sense—it was his home. Had he bought it after his wife died? Or had Sara helped?

Mandy spotted the kitchen and veered there to deposit the brownies.

It was when she walked back into the living room that she saw the photo—an eight-by-ten of a woman and child. Obviously Jackson's family.

With a quick glance at him, she walked to the picture and picked it up. Sara had had short black hair and dark eyes that seemed to smile directly at her. Sammy had been a darling little boy, complete with a cowlick in the back of his dark hair and a smattering of freckles across his nose.

"School picture. They got a joint one because she taught there and he'd just started kindergarten. Taken two weeks before they were killed," Jackson said tightly from behind her. "It arrived in the mail the day of the funeral."

Mandy fought down the ache that his words brought. Slowly she replaced the picture on the end table. "I'm so sorry."

"Yeah, everybody's sorry. Doesn't bring them back."

Mandy wished she could say something, but she did not have any words to ease his pain. Nothing would bring back his wife and son.

"I'd better go." She turned and started for the door. There was nothing for her at her trailer—no memories, few regrets and a lonely dinner. What did Jackson have? Not much more—poignant memories, a lingering regret over circumstances he couldn't alter.

"Want to eat dinner here?" he asked when her hand touched the doorknob.

Mandy glanced at him in surprise. Jackson had invited her to stay?

"It's not much, just spaghetti. Sauce from a jar, but lots of it. And garlic bread," he said. Standing across the room from her, he looked uncertain, lonely.

Her heart was touched. And she'd appreciate the company.

"Sounds wonderful."

Where had those words come from? Jackson wondered as soon as they'd left his mouth. What was he doing, inviting her to stay? From the smile that touched her lips, she was delighted. He was a fool!

"What can I do to help?" she asked.

He frowned. Damn, what had he started? "I can manage, unless you want a salad. I don't have anything for that."

"I do. How about I go and fix a salad and come back in about twenty minutes?"

"Fine."

Reprieve.

He watched her go, then headed to the kitchen. He got tired of eating alone night after night. He often called Jeff and the two of them threw something together. Mandy was just another co-worker—someone to share a meal with. No big deal.

As he began to prepare the meal, he tried to keep his mind blank, or focus on the day's meeting. It had gone well despite Deirdre and her flirtatious ways. Even the latest discovery about Andrews Tool and Die had been mentioned and dismissed. Windhaven had not borne the brunt of the embezzlement, J&J Construction had. The resort owners were satisfied with the way he and Jeff were handling things.

Mandy had been an asset, as she probably knew. He almost smiled when he remembered her clever trick, giving him an out for lunch. For that and the brownies, he owed her.

Dinner was simply a way to repay the favor. It wasn't as if they were going out on a date or anything. But dinner with a fellow worker, hell, he did that all the time with Jeff.

But Jeff didn't disturb his equilibrium. Didn't bring long-dormant interest and awareness alive. Didn't have his blood thrumming through his veins when he laughed, or glanced up with bright blue eyes.

Sara's eyes had been dark. As had Sammy's.

Mandy was nothing like Sara.

He sliced the bread, smeared garlic butter on both sides and wrapped it in aluminum foil.

For a moment, he couldn't picture Sara. He looked at the photo in the living room. There. She was there, as pretty as she'd ever been. As pretty as she would always be.

He couldn't forget her. They'd been together most of their lives. It felt like a betrayal to even think of another woman.

Move on, Jackson.

The words sounded so clearly in his mind he almost dropped the knife.

He had moved on. He'd sold their home, unable to bear staying in it with both of them gone. He had made a life for himself, working with Jeff on remote sites—sites a lot of other construction firms didn't want because of the challenges inherent in out-of-the-way places and the distances from home. Home was now this trailer. It went where he went.

If a man traveled lightly, he couldn't get bogged down in relationships, nor risk his heart again.

The knock on the door came too soon. He took a breath and went to open it and let Mandy in. Her smile was tentative, as if she wasn't sure of his welcome. He nodded, tried to remember the rules of polite behavior.

"I brought two bottles of dressing, not knowing which you'd like. But there are lots of good veggies in the salad. I like fresh veggies, but they're hard to get this late in the season."

"I don't bother with salads much. But this looks great. Thanks."

Her smile became more relaxed and she followed him into the kitchen.

"I thought we'd eat at the counter." It was less formal. Where he and Jeff ate. Less like a date.

"Fine. Shall I get the silverware?"

"In that drawer." He pointed and headed back to the stove.

In only a short time, Jackson served up the food, heaping plates with noodles and sauce.

"I know I'm eating for two, but this is about a week's worth of food," she protested when he set her plate before her.

"Eat what you want. I'm used to Jeff's appetite." Jackson's own plate was piled higher.

He took some of the salad, more to be polite than anything. Sara had been big on salads, too. Was that a woman thing? Pouring on the dressing, he ate without speaking. Mandy had put a lot into the mix—tomatoes, green peppers, mushrooms, celery, carrots and two kinds of lettuce. It was good.

She ate the spaghetti quietly, not speaking. After Deirdre's clinging and posturing that day, it proved a refreshing change.

But even though Mandy didn't speak, he was aware of her. Her scent, light and sweet, seemed to subtly infiltrate his space. Her skin was fair, with faint color just below the surface. She was still in her jeans and flannel shirt, but made them look sexy instead of functional.

He scowled and looked away. He was not thinking sexy!

Her hair seemed to dance around her head as she looked around, taking in everything about his home.

What did she think about it? It was more luxurious than her own, but still a temporary abode. No pictures except of Sara and Sammy. None of the knickknacks women seemed to favor.

"It's delicious," Mandy said after a while. "Do you and Jeff often eat together?"

"As often as not. It saves one of us cooking each night. I especially like it the nights he cooks."

"Because you take a walk to the lake every day?"

He glanced at her. "I like some quiet time after the workday." He hesitated a moment, then continued. "Sara and I always spent time together before dinner."

"That's a nice tradition. I expect you miss that routine." Her voice was kind, but not dripping with sympathy.

He nodded. When he was at the lake he could almost imagine Sara was nearby, would be coming to join him momentarily.

"What was she like?"

"Sara?"

"Yes. She was pretty, I can see that from the picture. She reminds me of someone, but I can't think who. Was she tall, short, what?"

"She was tall, five feet ten inches. When she wore high heel shoes, she was almost as tall as I am."

Mandy stifled a sigh. She'd always longed to be tall and svelte. Tall and thin and sophisticated—like Sara. And Deirdre.

She sat up. "Deirdre, that's who Sara reminds me of. They look a little alike, don't you think? And Deirdre is tall."

"No, I damn well do not! Deirdre is nothing like Sara," he said. It was preposterous. Yet after that knee-jerk reaction, he reflected. Maybe he could see how an outsider might think that. Tall, sleek black hair, slender—there was a superficial resemblance, maybe. Deirdre dressed with more sophistication then Sara ever had. And while there might be some slight physical similarity, there was none in attitude or personality.

"Umm, I think they look a bit alike," Mandy repeated.

She was not one to back down. Jackson nodded reluctantly.

"Maybe generally, in physical looks, but they are nothing alike otherwise."

The same way neither was like Mandy Parkerson. She was a unique individual, carving a life for herself despite setbacks and a wobbly start. How did she keep that sunny disposition with all that had happened?

He wished he knew more about her, without having to ask. He didn't want to give the impression he was interested in more than a employer-employee relationship. Maybe Jeff knew more about Mandy, Jackson mused. Had he himself forgotten how to talk with people outside of work? He suspected if he just asked the right questions, she'd open up and share without reservation. And without expectations.

Her hand reached for another piece of garlic bread at the same time his did. Her fingers brushed against his, and she jerked back as if she'd been stung.

He lifted the plate and offered her a piece, still feeling the fleeting touch of her fingers. He studied her hands—slender fingers, nails short and lacquered with clear polish. Not the red talons Deirdre sported. For a moment the thought popped into his mind: what would they feel like touching him?

Watching warily, she took a slice and put it on her plate. She seemed uncomfortable. He took his own piece of bread, trying to think up something to say to ease the rising tension. He had no business thinking of touching or softness or anything about the woman beside him. He should never have invited her to dinner.

"—every winter?"

Jackson looked away. What was she talking about? How had he lost track of the conversation?

"What?"

"What are you going to do when you shut down the site for winter? Do you build smaller projects in southern climates? Take a long vacation? Or do you just stop work every winter?"

"Jeff and I plan to stay in Julian this winter, to be near the site. Once the snow comes, the road into here will be impassable until spring. We need to get the trailers out before then. We'll use Julian as a base for winter. We have two satellite projects going. I'll spend some time in Boulder and Jeff will probably check in on the one in Pueblo. The winter months will pass quickly. The sooner we can get back on-site next spring, the better."

"I'm not certain yet where I'll settle. I've lived in Denver most of my life but I don't want to go back there. I always wanted to live in the country. A smaller town would be better to raise a baby, I think.

"As far as Marc is concerned, the baby is not his concern. He disavowed any knowledge." She would never forget how he'd reacted—demanding she get rid of it, swearing she'd tricked him, that he had no intention of tying himself down with anyone at this point in his life, especially a baby!

"But it is his?"

"Oh, yes. There's no doubt there."

"There's always DNA testing, if you need proof."

She nodded. "I've thought about it, but decided not to push the issue. If he wants nothing to do with the baby, so be it. I'm not going to force the issue. It saves problems down the road. And I can manage.''

''What if something happens to you?''

''That's my worst nightmare. That something will happen to me and this baby will be alone in the world. It's an awful feeling when you realize you have no family, no one to count on to help in an emergency,'' Mandy said slowly.

Jackson imagined that for someone raised unhappily in foster care, it would be a terrifying thought to contemplate for her own baby.

''Chances are you'll live to be ninety or older.''

''Hold that thought!'' she said, trying to smile.

''No grandparents, aunts, uncles or other family around?''

''No one. As I told you at lunch the other day, I'm alone in the world until my baby comes. Then we'll be a family.''

Jackson thought about his own family. He hadn't seen his parents since he'd sold his house. But he talked with them every few months. Kept in touch. Sort of. His brother was up in Alaska, but Jackson still dropped him a card now and then. And he had aunts and uncles and cousins scattered all over Colorado. If he ever needed anything, he had family who would rally around.

As they had when Sara and Sammy had been killed.

Mandy had no one.

For a moment a strong protective surge overtook him. He wanted to offer her assurance that she'd be okay. That if anything went wrong, she could call on him.

He stared at his empty plate, stunned at the very thought. A week before, he'd flat out said she needed to leave. Now he thought about offering help if she ran into trouble?

No way.

Dinner was drawing to a close. He'd thank her for the salad and brownies and send her on her way. In the future, late or not, he'd take his walk to the lake and revel in the solitary time before dinner.

"Great dinner, but I can't eat another bite," she said, laying down her fork and pushing the plate a little away. "Thank you for asking me to stay. It gets a bit lonely sometimes. Not that I'm complaining. I love working here."

"But you must miss friends."

"A little. I wrote them about this place. And I'll see them when I stop in Denver next time. How about you? How do you keep up with friends?"

He rose and cleared their places. "I don't—too busy with work." He'd cut off all overtures from his friends, swamped by their sympathy. It had been years since he'd left Fort Collins. He'd lost touch with almost everyone.

Except Marshal Andrews, Sara's brother, and look where that had gone.

"A person is better off on his own," Jackson murmured, running water in the sink.

"I agree. I know I can count on myself. Why make friends who will let you down, or turn on you?" She stepped up beside him, scarcely coming to his shoulder. Even though a wide band held her hair back from her face, short wisps of golden hair framed her face. He missed the frame of locks around her cheeks. He'd like to slip the band off and let her hair spring free.

She reached out to take a plate from him. "I can wash the dishes. It's the least I can do after that great dinner.

But you have to put them away because I don't know where they go.''

He shut off the water. She was standing too close. Her light fragrance filled the air. He could feel the warmth from her body, see the sparkling blue of her eyes.

He wanted to kiss her. Wanted to feel that feminine body pressed against him, her arms around his neck, her mouth opened beneath his. He really, really wanted to kiss Mandy Parkerson, until they both forgot their names or where they were. Forgot the past and the future and embraced the moment.

The thought scared him to death.

Jackson took her by the shoulders and marched her from the kitchen. Even through the flannel shirt, he could feel the softness of her skin.

Was he nuts? He felt flannel, that was all. Warm from her body, but cotton only. No silky soft skin. No texture like velvet.

''I'll clean up. You need to go home.''

''I do?''

''Get some rest. You look tired. Today was hectic. Tomorrow we'll have to play catch-up on what didn't get done today.''

The hurt in her eyes almost made him change his mind. Almost, but not quite. Not if he wanted to keep his sanity.

''Good night. Thanks for dinner.''

Her voice sounded bruised.

''Thanks for the brownies.'' He opened the door, impatient for her to leave. Wanting her to leave before he forgot himself and drew her into his arms. Before he shut off the lights and let the two of them go where the urge would take them.

Chapter Seven

Mandy walked back to her trailer feeling totally confused. What had just happened? She thought they'd enjoyed a nice meal together. But once finished, he couldn't get her out of his place fast enough.

Had it been the talk of friendship? Did he think she wanted more from him than a strictly boss-secretary relationship?

Maybe she should go back and clarify that.

She hesitated a moment, decided against it and continued to her trailer. Once she reached her temporary home, she did her best to put all thought of Jackson Witt from her mind. Expunge every memory cell. Forget trying to figure the man out. He was unfigurable!

But he had been right; she was tired. An early night would be great, recharge her for tomorrow.

Of course, trying to ignore the man insured that he was at the forefront of her mind. She remembered every word he'd ever said. Remembered being carried from the lakeshore, being scooped up when she'd fallen wading. Remembered the feel of his hands on her shoulders as he'd turned her away from the sink.

Remembered the play of light in the office when he worked. And visualized him striding around the site, hard hat on, directing the men and equipment, ruler of his own kingdom.

She was not going to succumb to fantasies about Jackson Witt. He'd made his position clear—very clear. *He still loved his wife.*

And Mandy was wise enough to know her own judgment of others was skewed. Maybe because of her upbringing, or maybe because of a defective gene. Who knew? But her track record wasn't impressive. He was not interested in her and she had no business wondering more about him.

How long would he grieve for his wife? How lonely he must be in the evenings, alone in that trailer. What were his plans for the future? Whatever they were, they wouldn't include her.

She had seven more weeks to work with him, that was all. Nothing to get excited about, and certainly nothing to count on. She was the only one she could count on. Marc had hammered that lesson home!

The next morning passed swiftly. Mandy had plenty to do, and thanks to a restless night, she was not functioning in top form. Grateful when the lunch break arrived, she hurried to her trailer. Making a quick sandwich, she sank onto the sofa, relishing the relief as she leaned back. She'd close her eyes just for a moment. Then she'd eat.

While she'd gone right to bed after returning last

night, she'd tossed and turned all night long, feeling afterward as if she'd had very little sleep. Only a small portion could be attributed to an active baby. Mostly she lay awake with restless thoughts about Jackson. She hadn't felt this way before and didn't know how to handle it.

It felt so good now, to just relax.

At one-fifteen, Jackson glanced at his watch for the third time. Jeff was on the phone. Mandy was not at her desk. In the week she'd been with them, she'd been prompt on every occasion. What was taking her so long this lunch hour?

He put on his hard hat and headed for the door. Jeff glanced up but continued to listen to the vendor on the other end of the phone.

The day was warm, the sun shining in a cloudless sky. The long-range forecast had predicted a storm later in the week. But with any luck, it'd rain on Saturday and be clear again by next Monday.

Jackson stood in front of the office for a moment, scanning the work site. Men went about their accustomed jobs. The crane had placed the last piling yesterday, Moose showing off his expertise for the visitors. No one slacked off on Jackson's site.

So where was Mandy?

Taking a breath, he turned and headed for her trailer. Had she just let the time slip away, or had something happened to her? Again?

He knocked and waited. Nothing. Knocking again, he called her name. Still no reply.

Trying the knob, he found the door unlocked. Opening it, he stepped inside.

She was sound asleep on the sofa, her feet resting on

a chair pulled in front of her. Beside her on the cushion was a plate with a sandwich. She had not even taken a bite.

"Mandy?" he called softly. She didn't respond.

He remembered when Sara had been pregnant with Sammy, how tired she'd been. She'd complained she could hardly wait for school to end each day so she could take a nap. Then she'd be good for the rest of the evening.

He lifted the plate from the sofa and took it into the kitchen. Walking into Mandy's bedroom, he paused at the doorway, scanning the tiny room. It was as neat as a pin. She obviously made the bed before going to work. There was nothing feminine or frilly about the room, and she had used the bedding the company provided. But the air held her fragrance, and the small closet spilled over with the pastel dresses she'd worn last week.

He drew the spread from the bed and returned to the living room. Draping it over the back of the chair, he reached out to shift her position until she was lying down. She mumbled, then fell quiet, still asleep. He slipped her shoes from her feet. With the jeans she wore, she probably didn't need a covering, but he covered her, anyway.

Her cheeks were slightly flushed, her lashes looking like dark semicircles above them. She seemed younger without that feisty determination facing him.

Slowly Jackson reached out and touched the shimmering blond tresses, soft as down. Gently he wrapped a curl around his finger, fascinated by the degree of softness. He would have thought hair that fine would have no body to hold a curl.

He unwound the curl and turned. What was he doing?

She was an employee. And one that had caused him more trouble since she'd arrived than all the others on-site.

He walked out and quietly closed the door behind him.

Heading for the office, he entered to find Jeff gone.

Quickly writing a note, he left it on Mandy's desk and left. He had work to do.

Mandy came awake slowly. She wished she could turn over and sleep in. But today wasn't Saturday.

Today was Tuesday. She sat up. Tuesday afternoon!

"Oh, *no!*" she wailed, jumping up and untangling herself from the spread. She stopped and looked at it. Had she brought that out? She didn't remember.

Looking around, she spotted her sandwich on the counter in her kitchen. She knew she'd brought it to the sofa. Slipping on her shoes, she had a sinking feeling someone had been inside her trailer. She didn't remember taking her shoes off.

She looked at the clock. It was almost three! Panicked, she dashed out of the trailer and almost ran to the office. If Jackson needed any excuse to fire her, this would give him a doozy! How could she have fallen asleep at lunch? She knew she had to be back by one.

Had someone come to her place? Had she slept through someone entering and then covering her with the spread?

She rushed into the office, excuses trembling on her lips. The place was empty.

Going to the window, Mandy looked out. She didn't see Jackson or Jeff, just the men working. She recognized one or two. The rest she hadn't sorted out yet.

Turning, she went to her desk. She saw the note before she sat down.

"Mandy—plan to stay late today. Take a longer lunch hour, we'll work past six." It was signed "Jackson."

She sat down slowly. Take a longer lunch hour?

He knew! It had to have been Jackson who'd covered her up. But if so, why hadn't he woken her, told her to show up on time or be fired?

Maybe it had been Jeff.

For the moment, she didn't care. Her job was still safe. She had to make sure that didn't happen again!

Of course, if she got a decent night's sleep, it wouldn't. She felt tired during the day, but her doctor had told her to expect that. Normally she could handle it by going to bed early at night.

She began to work, hoping she could get things under control before Jeff or Jackson returned.

It was late afternoon when Mandy decided to call the local doctor for an appointment. Her obstetrician had told her to have biweekly checkups as she moved into the last trimester of pregnancy.

She was able to get an appointment late on Friday afternoon. Hopefully it would not be a problem taking off early from work. She could always make up some of the missed time on Saturday.

When she noticed the men drifting by the office, quitting for the day, her trepidation rose slightly. Jackson would be back. Had he been the one? Or Jeff? She wished she knew.

Jeff entered the office and dropped a stack of blueprints on his desk.

"It's hot as blazes midday, yet the temp drops so much by this time of day I need a jacket," he grumbled.

The Family &
Adventure Collection...

We'd like to introduce you to the
Family & Adventure collection, a wonderful
combination of Silhouette Special Edition® and
Silhouette Intimate Moments® books.
Your 2 FREE books will include 1 book from
each series in the collection:

**SILHOUETTE
SPECIAL EDITION®:**
*Stories that capture
the intensity of life,
love and family.*

**SILHOUETTE
INTIMATE
MOMENTS®:**
*Roller-Coaster
reads that deliver
fast-paced
romantic
adventures.*

Your 2 FREE BOOKS have a combined cover price
of $9.50 in the U.S. and $11.50 in Canada, but
they're yours FREE!

Your **FREE** Gifts include:
- 1 Silhouette Special Edition® book!
- 1 Silhouette Intimate Moments® book!
- An exciting mystery gift!

Scratch off the silver area to see what the Silhouette Reader Service™ Program has for you.

Silhouette®
Where love comes alive®

YES!
I have scratched off the silver area above. Please send me the **2 FREE** books and gift for which I qualify. I understand I am under no obligation to purchase any books, as explained on the back and on the opposite page.

329 SDL DU33   **229 SDL DU4K**

FIRST NAME	LAST NAME

ADDRESS

APT.#	CITY

STATE/PROV.	ZIP/POSTAL CODE

Offer limited to one per household. Subscribers may not receive free books from a series in which they are currently enrolled. All orders subject to approval. Books received may vary. Credit or debit balances in a customer's account(s) may be offset by any other outstanding balance owed by or to the customer.

If offer card is missing write to: Silhouette Reader Service, 3010 Walden Ave., P.O. Box 1867, Buffalo NY 14240-1867

DETACH AND MAIL CARD TODAY!

BUSINESS REPLY MAIL
FIRST-CLASS MAIL   PERMIT NO. 717-003   BUFFALO, NY

POSTAGE WILL BE PAID BY ADDRESSEE

SILHOUETTE READER SERVICE
3010 WALDEN AVE
PO BOX 1867
BUFFALO NY 14240-9952

NO POSTAGE
NECESSARY
IF MAILED
IN THE
UNITED STATES

"It's amazing how nice the weather's been," Mandy said, wondering how to broach the subject of lunch.

"Yeah, well, I heard a storm is expected this weekend."

"Not Friday?" She didn't relish driving that dirt track in a rainstorm. It would become a sea of mud!

"Naw, Saturday I think. Jackson hopes it'll blow through fast enough to be dry again by Monday. I hope so, too." He looked at her closely. "You okay?"

"I'm fine." Mandy smiled brightly. "Why?"

"Thought you'd be winding up for the day. It's after five."

"Jackson left me a note, saying he needed me to stay late tonight."

"Why?"

"I don't know, but I don't mind. I took a longer lunch hour than usual." She almost held her breath, but Jeff said nothing. Darn, if it wasn't Jeff, she'd bet her last dollar Jackson had found her asleep!

"I would like to take off early on Friday, if I may. I have a doctor's appointment."

"Something is wrong," Jeff said, jumping to conclusions.

"No. Pregnant women get regular checkups. My obstetrician in Denver recommended a doctor here and I made an appointment for Friday. It's routine. Nothing to worry about. But I'll need to leave by three to get there in time."

"Fine. Let Jackson know."

She nodded, rather wishing Jeff would tell him.

"You two getting along?" Jeff asked.

Mandy nodded again. She thought they were. Didn't dinner at Jackson's place qualify as getting along? And so far he hadn't fired her for falling asleep in the middle of the day.

Jeff smiled. "I knew he'd come around. That boy isn't dumb."

Mandy hid a smile. Jackson most definitely was no boy!

She was glad to get Jeff's okay for Friday. She found it much easier to deal with Jeff than with his partner!

"Sonny caught a mess of fish yesterday, so some of the boys are throwing a fish fry tonight. Want to join us?" Jeff asked.

"No, thanks." She had no wish to get tangled up with the others on-site. Despite her nap, she wanted to go to bed early.

"Maybe another time," Jeff said, heading for the door.

Mandy was noncommittal. She could see the wisdom of Jackson's edict. She spoke occasionally with Bill and Tommy. But they sought her out, she didn't look for them.

Other than that, she was friendly, waved if waved to and smiled at everyone. But that was her limit of inter-action—totally superficial!

Except for her boss and lunch. And dinner. And a picnic.

Maybe he should examine that edict more closely on his side of things, she thought.

When he entered the office some time later, she almost forgot what she was doing. He looked as tired as she felt.

Did he have trouble sleeping at night?

"I didn't mean to fall asleep at lunch," she blurted out.

He shrugged and took off his hat, running his fingers

through his hair. ''Pregnant woman are tired all the time.''

Of course he'd know; he'd had a pregnant wife at one time.

''I appreciate your letting me work later tonight to catch up.''

''There's plenty to do, but it doesn't all have to be done between eight and five.'' He sat down and tilted back in his chair, gazing off at the wall opposite.

Mandy didn't know if she should ask what the project was he wanted help on, or wait for him to bring it up. She expected a scathing remark about keeping up with the work, or how those who sleep on the job don't stay employed.

Keeping watch surreptitiously, she waited for him to speak. It was some time before he brought his chair down on all four legs and looked at the messages stacked on his desk.

He still didn't tell her what he wanted to work on.

A little after six, he rose and crossed to the front of her desk, tossing a handful of messages there.

''Phone them in the morning for me. You ought to be able to handle everything. I'm going to call it a day.'' He turned and headed for the door.

''Wait!'' She looked at the notes and then at him, puzzled. ''Why did you want me to work late?''

He looked to the left, not quite meeting her eyes. ''I was thinking you can adjust your hours if you wish. Take a longer lunch to get in a short nap.'' Without waiting for her response, he opened the door and stepped into the twilight.

Mandy was dumbfounded. For days he'd been harping that this was not the place for her. Yet when she'd given him cause to fire her, he'd worked around it.

She didn't understand the man at all.

But she was grateful for his change of heart.

Change of heart? Could there be more to his gesture than just her staying on the job?

Dare she even think of such a thing? Granted, she was lonely and yearned for companionship. But she was too wary to give her trust easily.

Jackson had his own baggage to deal with. How would two such distrustful people ever find a common bond?

The next two days passed without incident. Mandy took two hours for lunch and napped, never sleeping as late as she had on Tuesday. Grateful for the consideration, she tried to thank Jackson and was brushed off.

What did she expect? He was not going to win the Mr. Congeniality award.

On Friday Mandy decided to work through lunch, to minimize the time she was away from her desk. It was half past twelve when Jackson entered the office.

"What are you doing here? Isn't it lunch hour?"

Mandy nodded, calmly continuing to work. "I'm working through lunch. I have a doctor's appointment this afternoon. Jeff approved the switch."

"Are you sick?"

"No, routine checkup."

He nodded and went to his desk. They worked in silence, though Mandy was intensely aware of him. Every time he shifted, she glanced up. His hair was mussed from running his fingers through it. She'd seen him do it a dozen times, and could anticipate the action now.

He moved with an economy of motion. She'd love

to just sit and gaze at the man, but carefully looked down lest he surprise her and catch her watching him.

"I could drive you in," he said.

"What?" She looked up. What was he talking about?

"I could drive you into Julian this afternoon. I need to go pick up some things we ordered at the hardware store in town. I could drive you at the same time, if you don't mind going in the truck."

"I don't mind riding in the truck. But I can drive myself. There is no need to put you out." Her heart skipped a beat. He was offering to drive her to and from Julian? She remembered how tongue-tied she'd felt at lunch and on their picnic. To be enclosed in a truck for the trip would make her crazy.

Yet the thought was tantalizing, too. Maybe they could recapture a hint of the friendly atmosphere she'd found at the beginning of their dinner the other night.

Or maybe they'd end up arguing, as they usually did.

"You'll be tired, and it'll be dark by the time you drive back. I'd feel better if I was driving. There is no reason to take two vehicles, anyway. It's a waste of gas."

When he put it that way, it made sense. Plus she'd feel better if someone else drove back after dark on that lonely road.

"Okay, then. Thanks."

"When's the appointment?"

"At four-thirty."

He rose and started for the door. "We'll leave at three forty-five. I'm going to get something to eat. Take your lunch hour. Doctor visits are covered." He paused by the door and glanced back at her.

"Why don't you wear that pink dress? We might

want to grab a bite to eat in town, before heading home,'' he said, before he stepped outside.

Mandy stared at the closed door in stunned surprise. Had he just asked her to dinner?

Chapter Eight

Promptly at three forty-five, Mandy left her trailer and headed for the office. She'd dithered all afternoon about changing from jeans to a dress, as Jackson had requested. Giving in, she hoped she wasn't making a fool of herself. But it was the least she could do, since he was driving her into town.

He was not at the office when she peeped in.

Jeff looked up. "Jackson said he'd be here in a minute. He had to check something out with one of the men. That storm looks as if it's moving in faster than we thought. I bet it rains before you get back."

"Good thing he's driving, then. I wouldn't relish tackling that road after dark in the rain."

"That truck of his will go through anything."

She heard its rumble out front and bade Jeff goodbye. Starting down the stairs, she felt the butterflies in her stomach again. Jackson stopped the vehicle at the bottom of the steps and climbed out.

She nodded calmly, hoping he didn't have a clue how nervous she felt, but every cell in her body seemed attuned to him. He had changed into clean jeans and a new shirt. His shoulders looked wide, solid, dependable. His dark hair was combed, but she knew it wouldn't stay that way if he got frustrated and combed his fingers through it.

His eyes were hidden behind dark glasses. Maybe it was just as well. She swallowed hard and went to climb up into the truck's cab.

Once she was seated, he closed the passenger door and went around to the driver's side. In only seconds they were off.

"Do you have a lot to pick up?" she asked, striving to calm her jangling nerves. The trip took forty minutes at best. Might as well start off with some polite conversation.

"If everything came in, the bed will be packed," he said glancing at her.

She waited, but he said nothing further. No comment about her dress, the order at the hardware store or anything else.

The minutes ticked by.

He cleared his throat. "You aren't expecting me to go in to the doctor's with you, are you?"

"Heavens no. You can drop me. When I'm finished, I'll walk to the hardware store and meet you there."

For an instant, however, she wistfully wished someone would go with her. That there was someone to share the wonder of the experience and rejoice with her in the coming of her baby.

Once again she regretted the fact that she had no

family. The birth of a baby deserved fanfare and celebration.

"I can wait in the truck," he said.

"No, I don't know how long I'll be. Julian isn't that
large. I can find the hardware store and have a nice walk
to boot."

"Fine."

The next twelve miles passed in silence. Mandy did
her best to enjoy the scenery, though it still felt as if
she were traveling through a green tunnel with the top
blown off. The trees were thick and tall, shading the
road.

She felt herself grow drowsy. She hadn't taken a nap
at lunch today since she knew she'd be leaving work
early. Now the soothing ride was having its effect.
Maybe if she just rested her eyes for a couple of moments...

"Mandy?"

Slowly she opened her eyes. Jackson was leaning
over her, shaking her shoulder gently.

"Wake up, we're here."

She blinked, then came wide-awake.

"Oh, I'm sorry, I didn't mean to fall asleep."

He made a wry face. "No harm done. Can't say my
scintillating conversation kept you awake."

"What conversation? You're the strong silent type."

His eyes danced in amusement. "You think?"

She looked around at the low brick building that
housed the medical offices. He didn't need to be so
close. She was awake. He could sit back on his side of
the truck and give her some breathing room.

Grabbing the door handle, she glanced at him. His
face was only inches from her own. She could see her-

self reflected in his dark eyes, feel his breath skim across her cheeks.

Mandy felt a curious sensation, as if she were floating. She couldn't look away. What would it be like to lean forward those scant few inches and brush her lips against his? To have him wrap her in his strong arms and kiss her like there was no tomorrow?

Yikes! She was hallucinating now. Kissing her was the last thing Jackson Witt had on his mind.

She scrambled to unfasten her seat belt as he leaned back in his seat.

"I'll meet you at the hardware store," she said, thrusting open the door and almost tumbling out of the truck. "I don't know how long I'll be. You'll still be there, right?" She glanced back, holding the door as a shield.

He nodded, looking somewhat puzzled.

Slamming the door, she turned and walked briskly up the short sidewalk leading to the medical offices.

Idiot! she berated herself. He would think she was totally cuckoo. He'd done nothing but wake her up, and her mind had spun the fantasy that sometimes came late at night.

She had to get a grip! Jackson had given her a ride into town, nothing more.

Mandy left the doctor's office happy with the report. She had gained a bit more weight than he'd wanted, but it was nothing to be concerned about. As she strolled down the street, she couldn't help smiling. The doctor had discussed planning for the actual birth. She had to decide soon if she wished to stay in Julian or return to Denver. It wouldn't be too much longer before she held her darling baby girl or boy in her arms.

She sidestepped around a couple in front of her, then

stopped a moment, suddenly attentive to what was going on around her. The sidewalks were full of people. She'd had no idea there were this many people in Julian.

"Excuse me, can you tell me how to get to the hardware store?" she asked a woman walking by.

"Jesse's place? Two more blocks down and then turn right on Summer Street. It's three blocks after the turn."

"Thank you. What's going on in town tonight?"

The woman looked at her in surprise. "Football, what else? We're playing Henley. The high school band and team will be marching through at six. Happens every time we have a home game with a big rival. Then everyone goes to the high school field to watch our team tromp the other."

Mandy nodded her thanks and continued along the sidewalk, alert to the activity surrounding her. There was a preponderance of blue and gold—the school colors? Pennants waved. Excitement seemed to build as neighbors greeted each other and sought curbside spots to unfold lawn chairs.

Cars were no longer parked on the street. A sheriff's car cruised slowly along, the deputy calling greetings to folks from his open window.

Kids ran around and older folks gathered in small groups, chatting.

If she moved to Julian, she and her child would become part of this. Maybe she'd have a son who would want to play football. Maybe one day she'd be on the sidelines, proudly watching him march by on the way to a game with a rival high school.

Reaching Summer Street, she turned and immediately noticed the difference. It was practically deserted. She saw the sign for the hardware store and beneath it Jackson's truck. The back was piled high, with a tarp covering everything. But she didn't see him.

Mandy drew her coat closer, feeling the brisk wind as it blew across the parking lot. She headed for the glass double doors of the building. Jackson came out just as she reached them.

"All set?" she asked brightly.

He nodded toward the truck. "Everything came in. It's still early to eat. Want to do something else first?"

"We could watch the parade," she suggested, curious about the customs of this small town.

"What parade?"

When she explained, he shrugged. "If you like. We'll leave the truck here and come back for it afterward."

Mandy and Jackson found a small niche on the main street that gave them a perfect view. Both sides were lined with people. The air was festive and laughter rang out from different groups.

Promptly at six they heard the beginning strains of a marching song. Mandy leaned out to peer down the street, feeling excitement grow. She didn't know a soul in town except for Jackson, but it didn't matter. She'd cheer the parade on with the best of them.

Another gust of wind had her shivering.

"You need a warmer coat," Jackson said.

"I'll be fine for as long as the parade lasts, then we'll be inside."

He stepped closer, sheltering her from the wind. Another gust had her shivering again. This time he opened his own heavy jacket and drew her back against the warmth of his chest, wrapping the edges of the coat around her as far as they would reach.

Which wasn't far, but Mandy felt blissfully warm and sheltered with Jackson's hot body at her back. She looked over her shoulder and almost bumped noses with him.

"Thanks," she whispered.

"I can't have you freezing to death. Maybe this wasn't such a good idea."

Just then the band came into view. At least twenty teenagers were marching proudly, despite the wind and cold. Their uniforms were navy blue and white and gold, their hats worn at a jaunty angle.

The crowd cheered and clapped, Mandy joining in.

"Know any of those kids?" Jackson asked.

She shook her head. "No, but isn't it fun? Maybe some day I'll have a teenager marching in the band. Or playing football."

Jackson was quiet, and a moment later Mandy wondered if he was thinking about his own son. Would he have played ball? Marched in a band? Or gone into computers and science?

"If you want to leave, we can," she said.

Jackson looked down at her in surprise. "Why would I want to go? The parade isn't over yet."

"I thought it might make you remember your own son."

"Yeah, it does. But life goes on, Mandy. I can't ever have Sammy with me again. He won't ever go to high school, play football or date. It's hard to accept sometimes, but I think I'm finally getting it. His life was short. It was great while he was here, but he's gone. I don't mind that these kids are doing their thing. The world can't stop because my son is no longer in it."

"Still, you don't have to watch."

"I'm okay."

Jackson had his arms around her, holding her against his chest, trying to shelter her as best he could. She should have worn a heavier coat. And sturdier boots. He felt responsible. Why had he told her to wear a dress? She would have been warmer in her flannel shirt, jeans and boots.

She moved against him, straining to see everything, almost jumping up and down in glee watching the simple, hometown parade. Embracing life with all her enthusiasm.

Her movements were starting to cause serious problems. He held an armful of warm, delightful femininity. And his long-starved body knew it.

For the first time since Sara had died, he wanted a woman. Not just any woman. Mandy.

The instant the thought flashed into his mind, a million reasons why he shouldn't also crowded in. She worked for him. He didn't want to get embroiled with anyone. He suspected Mandy was the type to feel deeply before she let herself become engaged in any liaison. She'd been hurt, and would never be open to the suggestion of a casual affair.

She trusted him. The irony ran deep. She trusted him, but could he trust himself?

The football team came into view, pretty cheerleaders leading the way. The boys raised arms above their heads, helmets concealing their faces. But the townsfolk knew their sons, and the cheers rose louder and louder.

A convertible followed, with coaches sitting up on the back, waving to the crowd.

Then it was over. The people began dispersing, most heading in the direction of the high school. In only a short time, Mandy and Jackson were back at the truck.

"That was such fun. Everyone seemed so excited for the team," she said, sitting back in her seat, fastening her seat belt. "I hope they win."

"A small town is like that. Everyone knows everyone else. And it'll be more fun for them to win on the home field."

"Denver was too impersonal. I think I'll stay here. Maybe I can get a job with the resort when it opens."

"Wait until you spend a winter here. You might change your mind," Jackson warned. "Any place special where you want to eat?"

"No. The diner is fine."

"I thought about a place on the edge of town. It's an old farmhouse that's been converted to a restaurant." He'd never been to it, but it would do justice to the dress she wore. And mean more than dinner at the diner.

He drew a quiet breath. Did he want it to mean more?

Chapter Nine

The farmhouse restaurant was charming, Mandy thought as she gazed around when they entered. The entire ground floor of the old house had been converted to a dining area. Small tables with two and four chairs were scattered around the old parlor where the hostess seated them. The original fireplace was operational and a blazing fire heated the room.

They were seated near enough to the fire that they could enjoy it without becoming too hot. Mandy quickly shed her jacket. The warmth was a welcome change from the bitter wind.

"This is lovely," she said as she gazed around. It was more elegant than anything she'd expected to find in Julian. Or, truth be told, more elegant than she'd expected Jackson to like. She glanced at him. He was staring at her.

"Do I have something on my face?" she asked.

He shook his head and reached for the menu.

She took her own menu and scanned the different selections, wondering about his look.

When they'd ordered, Mandy smiled shyly. "Thanks for bringing me here. This is such a treat."

"It's just dinner."

"One I didn't have to fix for myself."

"I thought you liked to cook."

"I do, but not just for myself. Don't you get tired of cooking for one?"

"Jeff comes over often enough."

"Tell me how you and Jeff got involved in this project so far from home."

"Far from home?"

"Aren't you two from Fort Collins? That's at the other end of the state."

"We're from there. It's not home. I take my home with me."

Now.

The word wasn't said, yet it echoed in the silence.

"Okay then, home is here. How did you two go into partnership?"

Jackson looked as if he didn't want to talk, but Mandy didn't expect to sit in silence throughout the meal. And she was genuinely interested in learning more about Jackson. And Jeff, too, she reminded herself firmly.

Jackson slowly began to tell her about their business dealings, and she hung on every word. Since she knew each of them, she could fill in the background beyond Jackson's terse comments. She knew exactly who had done what in the various projects, even though he didn't explain. There was no need. She had a good grasp of each man's personality. Jackson had more drive than

Jeff, but the older man balanced the partnership with experience and a definite patience in dealing with bureaucracy. It was interesting to gain a glimpse of their shared history.

Mandy and Jackson both chose prime rib. When the platters came, the amount of food was startling. Mandy knew she would never finish even half. But it was so delicious she dug in with an appetite.

She tried to keep the conversation going, afraid to let silence swamp them. She was conscious of Jackson on a level she'd never experienced before. He fascinated her. She knew the danger of that emotion. It led to wanting to know more about a person, which then led to thinking that there could be something between them. Yet as a moth is drawn to the flame, she couldn't stop pushing to learn more. To give in to that desire to learn as much about him as she could. Curiosity, maybe. But compelling nonetheless.

She didn't understand why he'd invited her out for dinner, but she wasn't going to ask. She took the opportunity to gaze her fill, studying him when he wasn't looking, enthralled by the way the flickering firelight cast shadows on his face. She absorbed his deep voice, letting it seep through her like mulled wine. And she gathered every speck of knowledge he chose to share.

She was no closer to understanding the man when they left than she had been when they arrived. He'd sheltered her from the wind while watching the parade. But his conversation during dinner stayed on a superficial level. He rarely revealed much of his own feelings and hopes. Yet he had shown her a tender side she doubted few had seen.

It was pouring rain when they stepped from the restaurant onto the old-fashioned porch.

"Oh my gosh, this is awful!" Mandy exclaimed when a gust of wind blew a blast of rain on them both, even beneath the shelter of the porch roof. She was relieved he would be the one to drive home in the downpour. What if she'd driven herself into town that afternoon?

"I'll bring the truck close. Wait until I come to get you so you don't slip on the walkway!" Jackson instructed, hurrying toward the truck, not waiting for her response.

For a moment Mandy's independent streak reared up. She didn't like taking orders any more than the next person. Then common sense took hold. Of course she'd wait. She would not risk harm to herself or her baby.

Once again a tendril of warmth sparked deep inside, that someone else cared for what happened to her—even if it was just getting safely to the truck.

The ride home seemed treacherous to Mandy. The low spots in the gravel road had already filled with water. The rain beat hard on the windshield, the wipers ineffective in clearing the deluge. The trees on either side of the road swayed and bent in the onslaught, making it seem as if they would come crashing down on the truck. She shivered, feeling sorry for the kids playing football in this downpour. Or would they have called off the game due to the weather?

"I never could have made it myself," she murmured after the truck splashed through another deep puddle. The wind gusted again, shuddering against the vehicle.

"It's pretty bad, but it could be worse. It could be snow. The county plans to pave the road but they wanted all the heavy equipment gone so their weight wouldn't damage the road once it's built," Jackson said. He seemed perfectly at ease maneuvering his truck through the storm. Swerving to avoid a fallen branch, he threw her a quick look.

Mandy could see him faintly in the illumination from the dashboard. Otherwise the darkness was complete except for the headlights slashing through the rain, swallowed by the night.

She tried to relax. If he wasn't worried, she wouldn't worry, either. She trusted Jackson Witt.

Blinking, she gazed out into the tempest. *She trusted him?* She'd sworn off trusting men. Of course, trusting him to drive them home safely wasn't the same as trusting a man with her heart and future. That wasn't in the cards, no matter how much she sometimes wistfully wished it were.

But if she ever dared risk forming an attachment again, Jackson would be the one she'd trust to do what he said and stay the course. Look at his continued devotion to his family, gone three years now.

Would he ever consider starting a new family? Finding a new love? Or was he like her, too hurt and battered by life to venture forth again?

It was late by the time they reached the construction site. The thick gravel on the road and access area was dotted with puddles. Branches and limbs from trees had blown down. Some skipped across the open area, driven by the wind. Mud was everywhere else.

Jackson drove the truck right to her trailer. "I hope this eases soon. The forecast said it'd blow over by Sunday. I'm counting on it."

"So there'll be no problem working on Monday?"

"Let's hope not. Wait there, I'll come around to help you in."

She took her key from her purse, to have in hand. When he opened the door, the wind blew through the truck, strong and cold. Mandy shivered and stepped out into the rain. They almost ran to her steps. She had the door open in no time.

"Want to come in for coffee or something?" Mandy asked, rushing inside and turning to hold the door. The trailer felt blessedly warm after their mad dash through the icy rain.

Jackson hesitated a moment, then nodded and stepped inside.

She had invited him to be polite. She hadn't really expected him to take her up on the offer. Now what? After watching him throughout dinner, Mandy had grown more and more aware of him and the long-dormant needs of her own body. It had become more difficult by the minute to remember her vow of noninvolvement. A sweet kiss. A brush of his hand. She fantasized about more.

She hung up their jackets and went to the kitchenette to prepare the coffee. She busied herself with grinding coffee beans, putting on the kettle, wondering what she had to go with coffee. Some cookies, maybe? The brownies were long gone.

She was stalling and she knew it.

Maybe he'd gulp the hot beverage down when she gave it to him and dash away.

Jackson sat on the sofa, looking at home in the small trailer, at ease. She could see him easily from the kitchenette. And she envied him. Her nerves were dancing in anticipation. The blood pounded through her veins. The low light set a romantic tone. She frowned. Surely he didn't think she'd set the stage for something more than coffee and good-night.

Mandy found a package of cookies, opened it and

placed a few on a plate, wishing she had made more brownies recently. Jackson loved them.

Wasn't that old saying the way to a man's heart was through his stomach?

She kept her gaze on the teakettle, willing it to boil. She was *not* trying to get to Jackson's heart. It was simply that, as a cook, she appreciated it when someone liked what she'd made.

When the coffee was ready, she made tea for herself and took their mugs and the plate of cookies to the living room.

"Looks good," he said, rising as she entered, and reaching for the mugs. He placed them on the end table and waited until she sat in the flanking chair before resuming his seat.

"Tomorrow is Jeff's birthday, did you know?" he asked.

"No, I didn't. I wish you'd said something earlier, I could have bought a gift in Julian."

"He doesn't want gifts. But the men and I planned a sort of party."

"What's a 'sort of' party?"

"It's a party—but no alcohol. We're holding it here at the site, which looks like it'll be a good thing if this rain keeps up. We've enclosed one section of the main building. If the rain hasn't leaked through, we'll hold it there. You're invited—if you want to come. A few of the guys will bring a girlfriend. Some of the wives who come down periodically will be there, so you won't be the only woman."

She started to ask if that would be considered fraternizing with the other workers, but wisely kept quiet. He'd invited her. That was enough.

"I'd like to come. What time?"

"Seven."

Jackson took a handful of cookies and slowly ate them.

Mandy contented herself with watching him and sipping the herbal tea she'd prepared. It was cozy in the warm trailer with the rain beating down on the metal roof. The wind gusted from time to time, shaking the trailer slightly, but she wasn't concerned. She was pleasantly tired after the long day. Even her jangled nerves were soothed.

It was quiet evenings like this she'd hoped to have once she married.

"Have you thought of a name for your baby?" Jackson asked.

"Not yet. I keep trying different ones out. Some sound great when a person is an adult, but too formal for a baby. Yet I don't want him or her to have a childish name when grown. Did you and Sara know right away what you wanted to name Sammy?"

"He was named for both our fathers, actually. My father is Samuel Witt, Sara's is George Samuel Andrews."

"And what did you pick for a girl?"

"She wanted Brittany. I wanted Heather."

"They're both pretty. I like Melanie. I guess I'll have to decide before long." Mandy sipped her tea. It would be fun to name a baby for a family member, to carry on tradition through the generations. Only she didn't care to carry on the tradition her own parents had left her.

"It's getting late. I should go," Jackson said, setting down his empty coffee cup.

"Thanks again for dinner, and driving me in to begin

with. I would have ended up staying overnight in Julian rather than face that trip back by myself,'' Mandy said.

She fetched his heavy jacket and handed it to him, remembering how warm it had felt wrapped partway around her earlier when they'd watched the parade.

"I enjoyed tonight," she said softly.

He started to speak, but instead swept her into his arms and kissed her.

Mandy was startled, then forgot everything except the delightful sensations that splashed through her body. His hold was firm, pulling her to his long length, molding her against the hard play of his muscles. She could scarcely breathe, but who needed air when pulsating pleasure pounded through her veins? Her own arms wrapped around his neck and she responded to the kiss with a hunger that had been building for days.

She felt totally enveloped. His warmth invaded and heated her blood. His kiss deepened. Her own response matched his. She couldn't believe this was happening. Did thinking a thing make it come true?

It was as if he was as hungry as she for touch and feeling and connection. Did he miss contact with others as she did? Or was this more—special, meant for her alone?

He stopped suddenly, pulling back.

She wanted to hold on, to clutch him close and never let go, but slowly she released her hold around his neck. She gazed up at him. It was his move. What next?

"I shouldn't have done that," he said, his gaze roaming over her face.

His thumb came up to slowly brush across her lips. Lips slightly swollen and damp from their kiss.

She almost cried when he touched her so gently. And

heard the apology in his tone. She didn't want an apology. She wanted another soul-searing kiss.

"Please don't say you're sorry," she whispered. Why couldn't he have enjoyed it as much as she? Why not want another? They were young, healthy, and not attached to another living soul.

He looked at her, his expression fierce. "I shouldn't be kissing anyone."

Mandy stood on tiptoe and brushed her lips against his, wishing she could do more. If he wouldn't kiss her, she'd kiss him.

With a short farewell, Jackson spun around and left. The trailer almost rocked from the slamming of the door.

Mandy hugged herself, feeling chilled to the bone with his abrupt departure.

Neither was attached to another living soul, but Jackson hadn't let go of one who was dead. Was that why he'd left so abruptly?

Jackson stood on the trailer steps, tilting his head back, facing the rain. The cold drops soaked his hair and face. His jacket absorbed the moisture at an astonishing rate, and would be soaked through before long.

He hoped the cold would bring him to his senses. The wind blew icy blasts down his neck. Slowly he drew in a deep breath.

What had he done? Given in to temptation without a thought to anything but his burning need to hold Mandy, to feel her against him, to taste her mouth and see if the undercurrent of sexual tension was mutual.

And if her response was anything to go by, it was.

He was a fool. Stepping down, he walked to his truck,

ignoring the rain, ignoring the puddles he splashed through. He had no business kissing anyone.

What about Sara?

Sara's gone.

He groaned softly, opening the truck door and sliding in behind the wheel. He knew she was gone. Had known it every day for the three years she'd been dead.

Time to move on.

He clenched his fists and pounded the steering wheel. He had moved on. He had fashioned a life for himself away from all he knew and loved. He pushed Sara and Sammy to the back of his mind during the day.

But at night, they were there—just out of reach.

He could close his eyes and see them. Doing so now, he frowned. There was nothing there. Then the image of Mandy's dancing curls appeared. Her smile. Her feisty determination when she argued with him. Her laughter when Jeff told a joke. Her blue eyes bright with expectation and anticipation.

Jackson snapped open his eyes and started the truck. He had to get home. See the photo of Sara, recapture her image in his mind. Not someone else's.

He couldn't forget Sara and Sammy. And he would never forget the endless days and nights of pain and loneliness when they had gone. His life as he'd known it had ended. It had taken him months to get back on an even keel, to function like a normal person. He couldn't go through something like that again, no matter how tempted he might be to kiss Mandy, to want to spend time with her.

Even if he were to give in, she deserved better. After the father of her baby had deserted her, she deserved to have a man who would love her and that baby when it came. Who would stand by her through thick and thin.

Not a burned-out guy who would be moving on once this project was completed.

He walked into his trailer and flicked on the light. It was cold. Sterile. Except for the picture of Sara and Sammy, nothing personal was on display.

Jackson contrasted it to the warmth of Mandy's trailer. He couldn't remember any personal items, but there was something about her place that cried home. His was just shelter from the storm.

He picked up the photo and stared down at the two people he'd loved most in the world. Sara looked so happy. She had always been happy. At least he had that to hold on to. And Sammy... How proud he'd been, going to school just like a big kid. He would have been eight now, in third grade. Jackson and Sara had discussed getting Sammy a dog when he was older. Eight would have been a great age to have a dog.

As Jackson stared into the beloved faces, he felt an easing of the tension, a fading of the old ache. They had been a part of his life, and he would always have the memories. But they were gone.

Time to move on.

He traced his fingers over Sara's cheeks. Cold glass met his touch. He touched Sammy's nose. Only cold glass. With a sigh, Jackson carried the photograph into the bedroom and put it in the top drawer. It was time to move on.

Mandy loved Saturdays best, she thought, snuggled down in her bed. She could sleep in as late as she wanted. Do a few chores, then take a nap if she wished. Eat when she wanted, and wear comfortable clothes.

So why did she awaken at six forty-five, her mind

spinning with images of Jackson Witt? She had to find some technique that would enable her to forget him!

Forget that kiss.

Might as well tell her to forget to eat. She doubted she'd ever forget that kiss. It was unlike any she'd ever received. He was unlike anyone she'd ever known.

And definitely off-limits. Stay away from him, she told herself, trying to fall back asleep.

Memories ended and imagination took hold. As she was drifting off, she could see Jackson forging a path through a crowded room, sweeping her away to a dark corner, kissing her until she couldn't remember her name. Or whisking her to a sunlit hillside, where the two of them would be alone on a carpet of wildflowers. Carrying her away with passion.

It was late morning when Mandy woke again. She refused to dwell on the erotic dreams she'd had, and set to work cleaning the trailer and baking cookies to give to Jeff at the party. At least she could contribute something.

Just before seven that evening, Mandy was ready. She wore her yellow dress and had done her best with her hair and makeup. She looked good, she thought, smiling at herself in the mirror. The sparkle in her eye was from the thought of the party, she told herself. The color in her cheeks came from the short walk she'd taken that afternoon after the rain had stopped.

The knock on the door surprised her. She quickly went to answer it. Bill Frates stood on the steps.

"Hi, Mandy. I thought I'd walk you over to the party. It's still muddy in spots."

"Why, thank you, Bill. I appreciate that." She put on her heavy coat, gathered the cookies and was ready.

The enclosed area of the new resort was huge. Two

industrial-size heaters were doing their best to warm the place up, but since tarps comprised a portion of the walls, it was a never-ending challenge. Still, she was surprised at how warm it was. Enough to take off her coat. She left it in the pile near the door.

Almost everyone who worked on the site was present, Mandy noted, plus a dozen or so wives and girlfriends. She spotted Jeff right away and headed over to greet him and give him the cookies she'd baked.

A three-piece band was at one end of the room, warming up. The plywood flooring would provide ample space for dancing. Mandy recognized one of the band members—Moose, the guy who ran the crane. Obviously the group was comprised of construction workers who liked to play.

"Mandy, glad you came," Jeff greeted her with a big smile.

She held out the bag of cookies. "Happy Birthday, Jeff."

"What's this?"

"You said you liked oatmeal cookies, so I made you a batch."

"They're my favorite! Thank you!" He leaned over and kissed her on the cheek. "There's lots of food on the table over there. And drinks are at the makeshift bar. Help yourself."

A young couple came to wish Jeff happy birthday, and Mandy drifted away, not wanting to be drawn into the conversation. She studied the skeleton of the building, noting the window openings where tarps held back the cold. The high ceilings with their exposed ductwork and conduits would be enclosed by the end of construction season.

What would this space be when the resort was complete? A ballroom? A convention hall?

She ambled around, smiling at those men she recognized, nodding politely to others who greeted her. Two stopped to introduce her to their wives.

The music was wild and fast. Couples danced, men breaking in and switching partners. Everyone seemed to be having a great time. Mandy strayed to the sidelines, near one of the heaters, enjoying the music and wistfully watching the people dancing. Her carefree days were nearly gone. In only a couple of months she'd be a mother. She'd have to stay home and care for her baby for a long time. Who knew when she'd attend another dance?

"Care to dance?" One of the younger men came up to her, already puffing slightly from exertion.

"Maybe later," Mandy said with a smile. Mindful of Jackson's first prediction, she had no plans to dance, but didn't want to get into a discussion. It was enough to smile and gently refuse.

"Sure." He grinned and headed off to find another partner.

Mandy looked around. Had Jackson not come, after all? Suddenly she spotted him talking with a group of men across the room. He glanced up then—directly at Mandy.

She felt a flush of heat and quickly looked away. She didn't want him to think she was looking for him.

Maybe she'd get something to eat and then leave. She walked to the buffet table and selected a few pieces of finger food. Nibbling, she wandered to where one of the men was holding forth as if he were a bartender. She watched for a moment, laughing at his nonsense, then ordered up the house specialty—Windhaven Windy—a mixture of cola and his special secret ingredient. Sipping it, Mandy thought the secret ingredient was lemonade. It was not the best drink she'd ever had.

Reclaiming her spot near the heater, she had scarcely taken another bite of her food when Jackson materialized.

"Dance?"

She looked up and her heart skipped a beat. "I don't think so. Too fast for me."

Then the melody registered. It was a slow, dreamy song, quite different from the fast-stepping rhythms that had been playing all evening.

"You can handle this." He took her plate and put it on the floor. Holding out his hand, he stood there, waiting.

Mandy took a deep breath and stretched out her own hand. When his closed over hers, she let her breath go. The magic she always experienced around Jackson invaded.

Trying to ignore the clamoring desire, she walked calmly to the cleared area and moved into his arms. She would not dwell on the memory of their kiss. This was a sedate, staid dance in front of the entire work crew. A duty dance.

A pang struck. Was it only a duty dance?

"Having a good time?" Jackson asked.

She nodded, her gaze firmly fixed to the left of his shoulder.

"Speak to Jeff?"

She nodded.

"Are you not speaking to me?"

With that she looked up and saw amusement dancing in his dark eyes.

"Sure. What shall I say?"

"Invite me in for coffee when this is over and we'll see what we can discover to talk about."

"Talk? Or something else?"

"Now, Miss Mandy Parkerson, what else could we do?"

She bit her lower lip, trying to keep from grinning in delight. "I might make some brownies. I know you like them."

"I liked dessert last night, too," he said, drawing her even closer as they moved to the music.

She admitted to being slightly surprised to find out what a great dancer Jackson was. She'd thought that, with him being stuck at construction sites most of the time, his social amenities would be in short supply. He danced better than anyone she'd ever danced with. They seemed in perfect synchronization, floating to the melody, in tune with the music and each other.

It was only a dance. She had to remind herself more and more frequently lately that nothing could come of a relationship between Jackson and her. But for a moment, just the tiniest moment, she wished something wonderful could develop. Wished they were two different people who could meet, fall in love and trust that the future would be perfect.

Instead, she was afraid to trust again. Wary of commitment by others. What would it be like to walk through life unafraid?

Jackson continued to stand beside her when the music stopped. Several of the men gave them curious looks, but he seemed to be unaware.

"Want something to drink?" he asked after a moment.

"Not the Windhaven Windy," she said firmly.

He looked puzzled.

"Tonight's bartender is coming up with wild concoctions instead of giving out plain sodas, and that was one. It was gross."

"I'll avoid that. I'll make sure he gives us plain cola, if that's what you want."

"Or we could have coffee at my place," she said daringly.

Chapter Ten

When he didn't respond immediately, Mandy wanted to sink through the floor. He'd suggested it earlier, but hadn't he meant it? Was he worried she planned to seduce him?

She looked away, afraid she'd burst out laughing. It was too ludicrous for words. She was almost seven months pregnant with another man's baby. Would anyone in his or her right mind think she could seduce a man at this stage? Especially someone like Jackson Witt?

"I should stay a bit longer. It's Jeff's night and I don't want to cut out early," Jackson said slowly.

"I understand." Mandy tried to keep her tone offhand and casual. She could feel the sting of embarrassed color in her cheeks. How soon before she could slip away and hide in her trailer?

"I think I'd like something cold to drink, after all. I

can get it.'' She smiled brightly and started for the makeshift bar. Anything to get away from the situation. Once out of sight, she'd make a dash for her trailer and stay there until Monday morning!

"I'll get it. You wait here." Jackson touched her lightly on the shoulder and headed for the crowd around the bar. Mandy debated dashing away the minute his back was turned, but knew that would give rise to speculation she didn't want.

She wished she hadn't so impetuously invited him to her trailer. He'd probably just been making small talk. In the future, she'd make sure she kept her distance. Jackson was her boss, nothing more.

When she saw him heading back, panic flared. Bill Frates joined her before Jackson reached her. Bill had invited her to join him for dinner several times. Mandy had always refused, but she tried to remain on friendly terms with him. And he obviously held no hard feelings. He'd escorted her to the dance to make sure she made it without mishap.

"Care to dance?" he asked.

Before she could frame a polite refusal, Jackson arrived and held out the cola. "She's sitting this one out."

Bill looked puzzled.

"With me," Jackson said firmly.

"Oh, sure, boss. Maybe later." Bill looked at each of them speculatively, then turned and strolled away.

Mandy sipped the cold beverage, glad to have something to do to cover her surprise. Jackson would give rise to rampant speculation if he continued acting like that. One would almost think his tone was possessive.

"This is nice," she said, casting around for a neutral topic of conversation. "Do you have parties often? Seems a good way for everyone to let off some steam."

''There'll be a big bash at the end of the season. Not all of the men will return next spring. Some will find other jobs during the winter. Others do winter work, like snowplowing, or working the ski resorts, and are ready to return to construction when the weather turns good. This party is an exception—for Jeff's birthday.''

The man of honor joined them just then and the three chatted as they watched the activities.

When Mandy thought a sufficient time had elapsed, she excused herself, claiming to need the ladies' room. Instead, she headed for the coats and dug hers out. With a wistful glance behind her at the festivities, she let herself out into the cold night.

She carefully made her way to her trailer. The mud was frozen in spots, still soft in others. The wind had died, and the chilly air was still. She wished she'd brought a flashlight, but she reached the trailer without mishap.

Inside, it was warm and cozy and quiet. Too quiet. She could still hear the music from the party.

She slipped off her shoes and prepared a pot of tea. She'd read for a little while, then go to bed. Tomorrow she could sleep in late and maybe take a walk along the lake, if the ground had dried up enough.

The baby must have liked the party, she thought a few minutes later as she settled on the sofa to begin to read a mystery she'd brought with her. Her child was actively moving around. Mandy wondered if it could also hear the music and was dancing.

A knock on the door startled her. Peering through the peephole, she saw Jackson. Mandy opened the door.

''I came for that coffee,'' he said.

She stood aside, butterflies dancing in her stomach. He'd come for coffee, but was that all?

Quickly she switched on more lights.

"Have a seat. I boiled water for tea just a few minutes ago, so it won't take long to reheat for coffee. I thought you wanted to stay at the party longer."

"I did. But I want to see you more. Why did you leave?"

"Oh." Mandy didn't know what to say. "It was time."

He shrugged out of his jacket and flung it over the back of a chair. "Coffee?" he said when she seemed glued to the spot.

Flustered, she turned toward the kitchenette. But Jackson stopped her, his hand on her shoulder. She turned slowly and looked up into his eyes.

"Mandy," he said slowly. Then he lowered his mouth to hers.

The bright lights should have dampened the mood. But nothing could dim the excitement of his embrace. Before she knew it, he'd wrapped her in his arms and deepened the kiss. His lips were cool from the night air. He tasted of cola and Jackson. His arms held her strongly, yet with a hint of tender emotion.

Wrapping her arms around him, she gave herself to the kiss. *Never question good fortune* was her last coherent thought.

He felt solid and hot and strong. The little zings of energy surging through her were delightful. She felt free and alive and brimming with passionate energy.

His tongue danced with hers. His heartbeat matched hers. Time seemed to stop then. Eternity was in his kiss.

He took a step nearer the door and fumbled for the light switch, flicking it off, leaving only the lamp by the table to provide illumination.

It was romantic, she thought fuzzily through the roiling sensations. The faint, distant music lent a fey quality to the night. They were alone in the world, just the two of them. In seconds all thought fled. Mandy was consumed by the fierce desire that raged through her. Consumed by the feelings and sensations she floated on.

Only Jackson had ever elicited such a response from her. Was the man magic? Or just very, very special?

They were dancing. She knew it as they moved across the room. Slowly, to some rhythm she could only hear in her mind. It was slow, sensuous, romantic. Wrapped in a world of two, Mandy wished the night would never end.

She was flying, floating—falling!

Opening her eyes, she saw that Jackson had lowered them onto the sofa. He cradled her, holding her safely against his chest, his arms still wrapped around her.

She should have pushed away, tried for some normalcy. Remembered all the hurts of the past. But his kisses made her hungry for more. His touch evoked desire that flamed out of control. His presence drove away all memories.

She wanted more. She wanted him!

The pounding on the door went unheeded for several seconds.

Finally reality intruded.

"What the hell?" Jackson glared at the door. The hammering was relentless.

Mandy pushed back, aware that her dress had ridden up, the skirt twisted.

"Should I see who it is?" she whispered, standing.

"No, I'll check it out." He swiftly crossed to the door, running his fingers through his hair. If he thought to bring order, Mandy mused, he'd missed the mark.

Jackson flung open the door. One of the workmen stood there, fist raised to knock again.

"Boss, there's trouble. Jeff's trying to handle it, but sent me for you. It's Moose. He's fighting with Bob and they're really going at it."

Jackson nodded, already reaching for his jacket. "I'll be right there."

Mandy stayed near the sofa, hoping she didn't look as disheveled and loved as she felt. She did not want to give rise to any gossip about herself and Jackson.

He looked at her. "I have to go."

She nodded.

"I'll be back."

Mandy said nothing, too conscious of the man watching them. Jackson waited a moment, then stepped outside, pulling the door shut behind him.

She crossed the room slowly, pushing the dead bolt home with a click. She was still breathing hard from their kisses. And her blood felt inflamed, warming every inch of her. Where would they have gone had the man not interrupted?

Rational thought began to seep in. She at least had held an illusion with Marc that there was a chance for happy ever after. She had none of that with Jackson. Did she want a short fling until the job finished? Or would that only end up hurting her even more than cutting things off now? She suspected walking away from Jackson would be far worse than when Marc had ended their relationship.

She knew herself. She was already feeling more for Jackson than was safe. Where was her lofty determination to stay clear of any association with someone new? Of all people to become entangled with—a man still in love with his late wife!

Mandy turned off the light and went to get ready for bed. She really hoped Jackson did not return. But if he did, she would not open the door to temptation again.

By the time Jackson and Jeff had settled things and sent everyone home, it was late. Jackson walked with his partner to the trailers. Without conscious thought, he looked at Mandy's. It sat in total darkness.

Not that he blamed her. Sheesh, show some finesse, he admonished himself. She'd invited him in for coffee, and he'd jumped her as soon as the door was closed.

"Until that fracas, it was a good party," Jeff said as they drew near Jackson's trailer.

"For most of us. Moose will regret it come Monday when I tell him I'm docking his pay for the damages."

"They weren't that extensive."

"I should fire him for bringing liquor. He knows the rule."

"If it happened any other time, I'd go along with you. But tonight was a party and some guys can't party without booze."

"Then he should have gone into town and found some action there."

"Speaking of action, I saw you and Mandy dancing," Jeff said.

"So?" Jackson grew tense. Was Jeff going to make some ribald comment? If he said anything about Mandy—

"Just it was nice to see. She's lonely, I think. She doesn't have any family, you know."

"I heard."

"I don't think she knows what she's going to do when the baby comes. She even talked about settling down around here."

"She told me that."

"Ah. Well, then. Good night." Jeff kept on walking toward his trailer. Jackson watched until the older man entered.

"What was that all about?" he asked softly. Jeff wasn't trying matchmaking, was he? If he were, the last thing Jackson wanted him to know was what had gone on in Mandy's trailer that night.

He entered his own, flipping on the lights. Once again it struck him as sterile and cold. He looked toward Sara's picture, then remembered he'd moved it. Not even that remained for decoration. Sara would have had the place fixed up, homey. Sara. He missed her.

Kissing Mandy had been dumb. Their relationship would never amount to anything. Surely she knew that. She wasn't weaving fantasies of happy ever after, was she? Not after a couple of kisses.

Hell, he had a resort to build. And other projects to monitor. Maybe he'd take a trip up to their site in Pueblo and see how the foreman was running things. The weekly updates via fax might not be covering everything.

It was an excuse to leave, Jackson acknowledged as he headed for bed. Putting several hundred miles between himself and Mandy Parkerson seemed wise at the moment. And once he returned, it would be business as usual—emphasis on the business part.

He had no intention of kissing his secretary again.

Despite the sunshine on Sunday, it remained cold. Mandy ventured forth for a short walk along the lake, but was glad to return home. She made headway on her mystery novel, but found her mind wandering from time to time, wondering where Jackson was and if he'd returned last night. Had he tried the door even though the lights were out? Or seen the darkened trailer and not bothered?

From time to time she glanced out the window. If she saw him, she could…what? Invite him in for coffee?

Feeling restless, after lunch Mandy began baking. So what if it was brownies. If she liked to make brownies, she would. Maybe Jeff would like some.

As if thinking about the older man conjured him up, he knocked on the door.

"Come in," Mandy said, hiding her disappointment that it wasn't the other partner. "You're just in time. I've made some brownies. They're baking now, and will be ready soon."

"Smells real good. I came to see how you were doing. I didn't see you go for a walk today."

"I went early, but didn't stay long. It's too cold."

"Yeah, that storm dumped a lot of rain, but it was ahead of the cold front, or it would have been snow. Another storm is due in later this week. I think our days here are becoming numbered."

"Did you enjoy your party?" Mandy asked, fixing them each something hot to drink—uncaffeinated herbal tea for her, coffee for Jeff.

"Until Moose and the boys started fighting. I didn't get a chance to dance with the prettiest girl there, however. Jackson beat me to it."

"Oh?" She would not be jealous. It didn't matter to her who Jackson danced with.

"You, I mean." Jeff smiled and winked.

"Hardly the prettiest one there." Mandy felt flattered that the older man took the effort to make her feel special.

She cleared her throat and tried to sound nonchalant. "Where is Jackson today? Not working, I hope."

Jeff looked at her sharply. So much for sounding casual.

"He left this morning for Pueblo. He'll be back later in the week."

"Pueblo?"

"We have a small shopping center going up there. We have a foreman running the job. He reports in weekly, but Jackson got some bee in his bonnet about wanting to check it out in person. If we can't trust Mick after all these years, we might was well hang it up. Did you enjoy the party?"

They talked about the party and the storm, and the accelerated schedule Jeff and Jackson planned to implement because of the last storm and pending ones already predicted.

But always in the back of her mind was the question of why Jackson had left. He had made no mention of it during the previous week. Or even Saturday night.

The next week seemed to drag slowly by. Mandy entered the office each day half expecting, half hoping to see Jackson stride in, his hair tousled from running his fingers through it, his eyes taking in everything, their dark depth giving away little in return.

Instead, his desk remained conspicuously empty.

Jeff handled the office questions, decisions and planning. He also spent a lot of time out with the men. The entire camp seemed focused on working longer hours, to get as much done as they could before buttoning up for the winter.

Mandy knew enough to run her part efficiently. With her naps at lunch, the days fell into a routine that was easily manageable. The nights were a little lonely, but she was used to those. As long as she kept her fantasies firmly in check, she was fine.

On Wednesday Jackson phoned. Mandy took the call. "Is Jeff there?" he asked. No hello for her.

"He's out on the site. Should I try to find him?"

"No, tell him to give me a call when he comes in. He has my cell phone number."

"Are things going okay there?" she asked.

"Fine."

She waited, but he obviously wasn't going to say more.

"Things are going fine here, too," Mandy said. Couldn't she think of anything else to say?

"Good. Have Jeff call." He hung up.

Slowly she replaced the receiver. What had she expected? More than that brisk phone call, obviously. She jotted the message for Jeff and tried not to feel hurt that Jackson had been so abrupt.

By Friday, the entire camp was talking about the impending storm. The weather had warmed up during the week, so snow wasn't a threat, but major precipitation and high winds were predicted.

"At least it'll strike on the weekend again," Mandy said to Jeff late Friday afternoon. The trees were already swaying in the wind. The sky churned with dark clouds. "By Monday it'll probably blow over, and everyone can get back to work," she said optimistically.

"I don't know, this one might last a few days. It's a slow-moving storm and has already caused minor flooding in Wyoming and the northern part of the state."

"Will the lake water rise?" Mandy had an instant picture of the entire site being engulfed.

"Not so we'd notice. I'm more concerned with the winds. We're battening down the hatches today, to make sure damage is minimal. But I wouldn't be surprised if we have some damage because of the high wind.''

''Isn't there anything else to do?''

Jeff shook his head. ''We've built it as strong as we can. This'll be a good test. Anything that doesn't hold up can be replaced.''

The wind came before the rain. Mandy was buffeted by it as she walked to her trailer after work. Gusting, it swirled leaves and small twigs around. She was grateful for last week's rain, which kept the dust down.

By the time she heated her supper, the rain had started, the drops sounding like hail against the metal roof of the trailer. The wind battered the sides, rocking the trailer slightly. She shivered after one fierce gust, grateful to be inside, warm and safe.

Going to bed later, she found the storm was not conducive to sleep. From time to time she heard a sharp crack as a branch fell from a tree, startling her. She stared into the darkness, straining her eyes to see outside. Except for a few pools of light from other trailers, the storm clouds obliterated everything.

Lying awake, she grew restless. Maybe she should try reading her book. She was close to the end and wanted to see if her guess about who the villain was would prove correct.

She rose and went to the living room to find the book. The light from the hall was all she needed.

Just then a loud crack sounded, as if it were right on top of her. The entire trailer shook, then cold air swooped in and enveloped her.

Mandy ran back to the bedroom, stopping in the doorway in horror. A tree had smashed across the end of her trailer, ripping a gash in the roof and side. Rain swirled in, cold and wet. Her bed was covered in branches and pine needles.

She grabbed her bathrobe from the nearby chair and put it on. Fumbling for her sneakers, she got them on, too. All warmth had fled. Rain was soaking the carpet, blowing onto the bed. The light was off, but illumination from the hall enabled her to determine the damage. It looked as if the entire back corner of the trailer had been crushed.

There was no way she could spend the night in the room. Rain would have everything sopping wet in minutes. And she wouldn't trust the tree not to shift and settle even more.

She started for the living room and then reconsidered. With a wary eye on the tree, she got a clean pair of jeans and a couple of shirts, then hurried from the bedroom. Dressing quickly, she went to assess the damage one more time. The rain, driven by the wind, had not abated. Everything was soaked. The blow had shattered the windows. Pieces of tree limbs, bent metal and glass dusted the floor, the bed, the dresser.

She put on her heavy jacket. Forget about an umbrella; it wouldn't stand a chance in the wind. She wished she had a cell phone. She hated to go out into the rain, but needed help.

Hurrying through the mud and rain, she banged on the door to Jeff's trailer. He opened it seconds later. When he recognized her, he practically pulled her into the trailer.

"Mandy, what's wrong? What the hell are you doing out in this storm? You're not having the baby, are you?"

Mandy shook her head, grateful for the warmth.

"No. A tree crashed through my bedroom. There's a

huge hole in the ceiling and wall, and rain is pouring in. I can't stay there. It's freezing in the trailer."

"You're not hurt, are you?" His concern was immediate.

"No, I was in the living room when it hit. Thankfully. There are two branches on the bed right where I would have been." She shivered, aware for the first time how close she'd come to possibly being injured. Or worse.

"Stay here, I'll get dressed and see what I can do."

"I'm not sure anyone can do anything tonight. Everything's getting wet. It's pouring out there." In the short time it had taken her to run from her place to his, her hair had been drenched and the shoulders of her jacket soaked.

"Take off your jacket. I'll bring you a sweatshirt from my room. And a towel for your hair."

Jeff came from his bedroom a few moments later, fully dressed and wearing a yellow slicker. He handed her a large sweatshirt and hand towel. Mandy gratefully pulled on the first and then began to dry her hair.

"You wait here. I'll be back after I assess the damage," he said, heading for the door.

She nodded, glad to comply. The storm was frightening enough without having to go out in it again.

By the time Mandy had her hair mostly dry and had warmed up, Jeff returned, Bob and Tommy with him.

"We've managed to cover the things in your bedroom with tarps, and tie them down. What's wet will have to dry out when the rain stops. We closed the bedroom door, so the rest of the place will stay dry. We need to cut away the tree before we can assess the damage fully. Can't do that until morning at the earliest."

"Do you think any more trees will fall?" She felt

vulnerable. What if a tree fell right across the living room when she was sleeping?

Another sharp crack sounded. A moment later the ground shook slightly as another tall tree fell. Tommy popped outside with his flashlight. He returned a moment later. "Couldn't see anything. Must have been farther away than it sounded. Some of the other men are out. One of the campers near the lake got hit by falling branches."

"Do you have what you need for the night?" Jeff asked.

Mandy looked surprised. "Shouldn't I return home?"

"I'd feel better if you spend the rest of the night here. You can have my bed. I'll catch some sleep on the sofa if I get a chance. First, I'm going back out to see what else has been damaged. Your place won't hold the heat, anyway, with that gash. No sense wasting propane trying."

"I can't take your bed," she protested. "I can use the sofa."

"I'll be out for a while, honey. You get some rest. Fresh sheets are in the small closet by the bathroom."

Jeff and the others left. Mandy made up the bed with fresh linens and gratefully climbed into it. She took off her shoes and jeans, keeping everything else on. She was still a bit cold and the sweatshirt felt good. In seconds, she drifted to sleep.

It was a troubled rest, however, for she was jarred awake every time she heard a limb break off, or the wind rocked the trailer.

She awoke near dawn to use the bathroom. Peeking into the living room afterward, she saw Jeff fast asleep on the sofa. The rain still hammered the trailer. The wind gusted, rocking the trailer gently. At least it hadn't been tipped over, she thought gratefully.

Quietly she crept back to bed.

A chirping sound woke her a couple of hours later. She looked around, wondering what it was. Spotting Jeff's cell phone on his dresser, she rose to answer it.

"Hello?" she said, still feeling half-asleep.

There was silence on the other end.

"Is anyone there?" she asked.

"Mandy?" Jackson's tone was incredulous.

"Yes." She went back and got into bed, pulling the covers over her legs. It was too cold to stand.

"Where's Jeff?"

"He's still asleep. Do you want me to wake him, or can he call you back?"

"Busy night?"

"I'll say! How did you know?"

"Put Jeff on." His voice had become icy.

Mandy frowned. "Okay." She kicked off the covers and pulled on her jeans. Fastening them as she headed for the living room, she wondered what was so urgent that Jackson wanted to wake Jeff. It was Saturday. Didn't the man ever take a day off?

"Jeff?" She shook him gently. "Jeff, Jackson wants to talk to you." She shook him harder. He groaned and rolled onto his back, gazing up at her through half-closed eyes. "Tell him I'm still asleep."

"I tried." She handed him the phone and went to the kitchenette. It was larger than hers, and well equipped. She found coffee and began to prepare it. There was no tea. One cup wouldn't hurt, she rationalized, trying not to listen in on Jeff's side of the conversation. Of course mumbled, half-asleep yeahs and nos weren't very revealing.

She saw Jeff sit straight up. "What the hell are you talking about?" he almost yelled.

Fascinated, Mandy forgot about being discreet. Had something happened at the site in Pueblo?

Jeff quickly recounted the events of last night, how she'd come to stay in his trailer, and included a report of damages she hadn't been aware of.

He waited a moment, then his tone softened. "That's all right. When are you coming back? We could use some help here.... I don't know, one of the men was going to try to get to Julian today. We need more chain saws than we have. It's a mess...." He looked at Mandy. "I'll offer. What happens when you get here...? Okay. See you then." Jeff clicked off the phone and lay back down.

"Is that coffee I smell?" he asked.

"It should be ready in another minute or two. Is something wrong in Pueblo?" she asked.

"No. The storm has barely reached them. And the wind doesn't seem as bad."

She couldn't very well ask what had gotten Jackson so agitated. She and Jeff weren't that close. If he wanted her to know, he'd tell her.

"Good."

When she handed him a cup of coffee later, she sat gingerly on the edge of a chair. "Are you going to be able to get rid of that tree in my trailer today?"

"I don't know. We're going to try."

"I don't want to put you out again tonight. I can sleep in my living room if I have to."

Jeff looked at her curiously. "Actually, Jackson suggested you bunk in with him."

Chapter Eleven

"What?" Surely Mandy hadn't heard him correctly.

"He has an extra room. Might make some sense—just until we fix your trailer. Think about it at least."

She opened her mouth to refute the idea, then closed it. What could she say that wouldn't raise suspicions?

Suddenly it occurred to her that maybe Jeff couldn't get up with her standing there. She had no idea if he slept in pajamas, boxers or nothing at all.

Making a vague excuse, she hurried into the bedroom, trying to think what she could do about her accommodations. Not until she heard the bathroom door shut did she venture out again.

Could she move into Jackson's trailer even temporarily? No matter how short term, it was definitely a bad idea. She couldn't control her fantasies when eating dinner with the man. However would she cope, actually living under the same roof with him? They would share meals, living quarters. And every night she'd know he was only the thickness of a wall away. She'd go crazy!

Sipping her coffee, she gazed out the window at her trailer, studying the massive pine lying at a steep angle across the roof. Branches covered it like a thick, lacy tablecloth. The top of the tree hovered over Jeff's trailer, but hers kept it from falling onto his. By craning her neck, she could see farther along the line of trailers toward the lake.

Branches littered the ground. Rain pelted puddles six feet wide. The trees continued to bend and sway in the strong wind. Watching them, she was amazed more hadn't fallen. They seemed to bend more than she would have thought possible. At what point would they snap and break like the one on her trailer?

Jeff joined her a few minutes later. The older man had shaved and dressed, but still looked tired.

"How bad is it out there?" she asked.

"No one was hurt, but there's a lot of debris. Branches, mostly. A couple of trees. Once we get the one on your trailer cut away, we can assess the damage. Same with Joe Porter's. It sustained heavy damage."

"If you can seal off the bedroom so the place will hold the heat, I can make do sleeping in the living room. The sofa is comfortable, and it's only for another month. I don't need to stay in Jackson's trailer. What happens when he returns?" Mandy said, wondering if they would keep her on if she had no place to live. She didn't relish making the thirty-mile trip from Julian each day—especially if the weather was anything like today.

"We'll have to see how bad the damage is. If the propane lines were cracked, or the electricity compromised, the place might be uninhabitable. Jackson has the room."

"While he's gone, you mean?"

Jeff cleared his throat. "Not only that. He has a bigger trailer than the rest of us—two bedrooms."

Mandy grew suspicious. "Is he coming back?"

Jeff nodded.

"And I'm to stay there with him?" Mandy didn't know whether to yell with frustration or quietly accept what looked like the way it was going to be.

"Plan to stay there at least until we know what to do with your place."

"And this won't give rise to problems with the men?"

"What are you talking about?"

"Jackson didn't want me working here at all, if you'll remember, because my presence would prove disruptive. This wouldn't prove disruptive?"

Jeff's eyes twinkled. "Only to Jackson, I suspect. And it serves him right. It's good to see the man take an interest in something beyond the job at hand. Plan to stay a day or two. We'll be better able to assess the repairs needed once we get the tree removed."

It would serve the man right if she disrupted every aspect of his life, because he sure had disrupted hers. For a moment, the thought made her smile.

She could be the perfect guest. He'd never know she was there. And if he wanted more kisses—well, he could find them elsewhere. She would not give in. And as soon as her trailer was ready, she'd move back so fast his head would spin.

At least that was her intention, until she actually packed up the few things she needed and headed for his trailer. Most were damp, and she went to hang them to dry in Jackson's bathroom, then stopped dead. The man had a tub!

Visions of a warm bath had her smiling in delight. Staying with Jackson would bring definite perks, especially when he wasn't even home.

After dinner, Mandy filled the tub with hot water. She'd carefully refrained from spending the entire day soaking in the tub. There were limits! Instead, she'd spent the day at the office, keeping track of reports of damage and repairs, and reporting to Jeff each time he came in. But lingering in the back of her mind was the lovely thought of the hot bath she'd have this evening.

By the time she'd prepared dinner, Jackson had still not returned. Maybe he was waiting for the next morning, when it would be easier to navigate the muddy access road.

She'd made up the bed in the guest room, and hung up her clothes, which had dried. Carefully closing the bathroom door and locking it just in case Jackson arrived home while she was using the tub, she slipped into the steaming water.

Bliss!

She soaked until the water turned cool, added more hot and stayed a bit longer. By the time she climbed from the tub, Mandy was relaxed and warm through and through. She put on her long flannel nightgown and matching robe, dried her hair, then tidied up the bathroom. Except for the steamy air carrying the scent of her bubble bath, the place was as she'd found it.

She opened the door and knew immediately that Jackson had returned. She hadn't heard him, but she felt his presence.

Tightening the belt on her robe, she hoped it covered everything. But with the mound of baby in front, she couldn't check below her waist.

''Mandy?''

So much for the burgeoning hope that she could dash to her room and pretend to be asleep. Facing him in the morning when fully dressed sounded wiser than tonight in her gown and robe!

''You're home,'' she said brightly. Clutching her clothes in her arms, she walked down the short hall to the living room.

He seemed to fill the space in this large trailer as much as he did in her own, smaller place. Her heart gave a skip. She'd missed him! Gone a week and she'd missed him every moment.

The realization struck with the impact of a cement piling. What would she do when the job was over and she never saw him again? Would she miss him the rest of her life?

The mere thought scared her. He could not become that important to her!

But she feared he had.

He looked tired. She wanted to wrap her arms around him, sooth away the stress and provide comfort. Blinking, she tried to black out the image.

''How are things in Pueblo?'' she asked, determined not to give in to the embarrassment that hovered. It was a good thing he couldn't read minds.

''Everything's progressing on schedule. How are you?''

''Fine.'' She smiled again, hoping this inane conversation would be the extent of their interaction tonight.

He crossed the room until he was almost touching her, crowding her, seeming to take the oxygen from the air. Raising his hand, he wound a curl around his finger, tugging gently.

"I saw your trailer. Thank God you weren't in bed when the tree came through."

She nodded, unable to say a word. Her senses were on overload, all from a gentle caress of a finger in her hair! She was aware of every nuance of his expression, the shadows in his eyes.

Clearing her throat, she tried to speak. "Can it be fixed?"

"I don't know. They were still working on getting the tree cut away when I arrived. They've stopped until morning. Is the guest room okay?"

She nodded, pulling against his finger. Mandy placed her palm against his chest and pushed slightly. Slowly he unwrapped the curl. She could feel the heat of his body through the shirt, the pounding of his heart. She snatched her hand back.

"Jeff said I should stay here. And I'll do it because I don't have much choice, but we'll be roommates, nothing more," she said firmly. She needed to get that cleared up so there'd be no misunderstanding on either side.

He hesitated, then nodded once and stepped back. "Of course. Do you have everything you need?"

"Yes. I'm heading for bed now."

"Good night." He turned and walked into the kitchen. Mandy waited for something more, but she heard only the sound of the rain on the roof and water running in the sink.

Disappointed that he hadn't challenged her edict, she turned. When she reached her room she dumped her clothes on a chair and took off her robe.

What had she expected—that he would be so overcome with desire he'd brush aside her words and sweep her into a passionate embrace?

Ruefully, as she slipped between the covers, she admitted to herself that was exactly what she had wished would happen.

What had he expected? Jackson wondered as the water poured down the sink. That she'd leap into his arms and beg him to make love to her?

He gave a harsh laugh. She'd never done anything to indicate she wanted anything more than a boss-secretary relationship. He was the one who had kissed her.

But she responded, came the whispered reply.

He shut off the tap, the coffeepot long since filled. Slowly he went through the motions of making coffee. Mandy was in the room down the hall, by now in bed. What did she wear to bed, something frilly and sexy? Or flannel, long and virginal? With her robe so tightly wrapped, he hadn't a clue.

Most people might not associate virginal with a woman who was seven months pregnant, but she had an aura about her that spoke of innocence and shyness.

He started the coffeemaker, feeling anger at the man who had gotten her pregnant and then abandoned her. How could anyone do that—to someone as sweet as Mandy?

Sweet? Not when she was on a roll about something. Not when she stood up for herself or something she believed in.

But there was an overall sweetness about her that drew him like a moth to flame.

And was likely to produce the same result. If he weren't careful, the barriers would crumble and he'd be as exposed as he'd been when Sara and Sammy were taken.

He rested his forearm on the cabinet and leaned his

head against it. He was tired. Came from not getting a good night's rest in a week.

He'd thought—hoped—the distance from Mandy would help him forget. Help him not yearn to kiss her, touch her, feel the silky texture of that beautiful blond hair. He'd hoped distance would allow him to gain some perspective.

Instead, he'd tossed and turned every night, wondering what she'd done during the day and what she was doing at that moment.

He didn't want to even think about his reaction that morning when she'd answered Jeff's phone, sounding so sleepy. He'd known instantly he'd wakened her. But the searing pain that hit at the thought of her in bed with Jeff had been totally unexpected. And not easy to erase.

Granted, Jeff was old enough to be her father, but sometimes women went for older men.

It wasn't as if Jackson had anything to offer her. Why should he care if Mandy found someone else?

"Someone else?" he muttered, straightening and taking a cup from the cupboard. The coffee was almost ready. "As if she and I had something going on and she was turning away."

He'd had his shot at happiness. Stolen away by a gunman's bullet.

Mandy deserved her own chance at happy ever after—and satisfying his needs and urges wasn't anything that would lead to that happy ending.

Jackson took his cup and wandered to the large living-room window, staring out into the stormy night, all his senses attuned to the room next to his bedroom. Was she already asleep? Should he knock on the door and tell her he didn't want to be roommates, that he wanted something more for the few weeks they'd remain on the job site?

And then what? Thanks for the memories? Have a good life?

He sighed and sipped the hot beverage. Life sucked sometimes.

Mandy awoke early Sunday morning. It took a couple of moments to realize where she was. Rising, she wondered if Jackson was still asleep. She opened her door slowly. The door to his room was shut. She quietly used the bathroom, then dressed. Venturing out into the main part of the trailer, she found it empty.

There was coffee in the pot, still hot. He must have gotten up before her. Was he already out? Or had he gone back to bed?

Mandy had brought her tea and quickly made herself a cup. She debated fixing breakfast for them both, but decided that, without knowing what he liked, or even when he'd want it, doing so would waste food.

By ten o'clock she was bored. The high winds had abated and the torrential downpour eased. Rain was drizzling down. Gray skies looked depressing. Jackson had to have gone out. There was no sound from his bedroom.

Finally she decided she needed some company. Donning her jacket, she headed for the office.

Several men were gathered around, looking up in surprise when she entered. Jackson was at his desk. Jeff leaned against the wall, talking with the group.

"Anything wrong?" Jackson asked.

"No. I just wanted to see if I could do something to help."

"The rain has stopped. We should have the tree removed by the end of today," Jeff said. "Pull up a chair. We're rehashing all that's gone wrong and trying to come up with a plan to get us back on track."

She hung up her coat and moved to the seat one of the men vacated for her. Smiling in thanks, she sat, her gaze going immediately to Jackson.

It felt right.

The thought scared her, but she couldn't help it. Being with him was what she wanted, even if she just sat on the sidelines and watched him. And she had the perfect excuse when he talked. Everyone else was looking at him, as well. No one would think anything of her own hungry gaze.

By the time the meeting broke up, Mandy had her emotions firmly under control. She had her own assignments from the discussion that she could start in the morning.

In the meantime, there was the afternoon to get through—and the evening.

When the other men filed out, she looked at Jackson. "I'm going back to fix some lunch. Shall I fix it for you, too?"

His gaze caught hers, held. "That would be nice."

She nodded, almost giddy with the thoughts that spun round. She wanted to push Jeff from the office, lock the door and get Jackson to kiss her again.

Instead, Mandy donned her coat and hurried from the place. The damp air felt good on her heated cheeks.

By the time Jackson stepped into the trailer a little later, Mandy had lunch ready. Thick ham-and-cheese sandwich wedges filled the plates, with apples and carrots cut in bite-size pieces. There were brownies for dessert.

"You don't have to fix all the meals," he said as he sat at the table with her.

"Lunch certainly isn't a problem. Consider it compensation for staying here."

He took a bite of a sandwich and chewed thoughtfully. "Your compensation for the job includes housing. Until your own place is fixed, this is housing. No need to pay for it."

"Okay. But I don't mind."

When they finished eating, Jackson carried the plates into the kitchen and ran water on them.

"I can do the dishes," Mandy said, following him in, carrying their beverage glasses. She placed them in the sink, bumping into him gently.

He seemed to freeze, then turned slowly. The water ran from the faucet. He ignored it as he put his wet hands on her shoulders and leaned over until his mouth covered hers.

Mandy sank into the kiss as if she'd been waiting for it all her life. His mouth was warm and sexy, bringing her alive as she'd never been before. His lips were firm and demanding, but not for more than she was willing to give. She hungered for the excitement being with him brought. Longed for the kiss to go on forever.

"Ah, Mandy," he said softly, gathering her closer, wrapping his arms around her, holding her snugly against him. Despite the baby between them, she felt as if she belonged just where she was.

Opening her mouth, she kissed him back, wishing she could burrow right under his skin and become a part of him. It was glorious kissing Jackson Witt. She reveled in the sweet, hot tingles of delight that coursed through her.

When he cupped her breast and gently rubbed the tip,

she felt the shock to the center of her being. Warmth invaded. Longing and hunger grew. She wanted more. She wanted Jackson. Wanted his touch, his taste, his unique scent. Wanted him to envelop her, fill her to the brim.

Her own arms were wrapped around his neck, giving him easy access. His thumb slowly, lazily brushed back and forth, each foray sending more and more molten desire to her secret places.

"I want you," Jackson said, breaking the kiss.

"I want you, too," she whispered.

His hand dropped to her swollen belly, caressing it gently. "It won't be a problem, will it?"

She shook her head. Her doctor had told her it was safe to have sex until just before the baby was born. Mandy hadn't paid much attention after Marc left, never imagining she would want another man, certainly not with the intensity she longed for Jackson.

He kissed her again, moving to nibble at her jaw, smooth her hair back from her face, tangle his fingers in the curls. His mouth never left her, brushing kisses along her cheek, then her mouth. Deep drugging kisses that had Mandy forgetting everything she'd ever known. The only reality was being in his arms.

He turned off the water and began to slowly back her out of the kitchen, down the hallway, never lifting his mouth from hers, his hands caressing.

When they reached his room, he fumbled for the door and flung it open. It bounced against the wall.

The sharp crack caused Mandy to jump in surprise. It reminded her for a second of the tree falling. She felt as if she were falling—falling in love with the most unsuitable man in the world. A man who had no inclination for romance or commitment. And who certainly didn't want a child cluttering a relationship.

But for the moment, she didn't care. He wanted her, she wanted him and it was glorious.

"Maybe I should get in bed first," she whispered when they were beside it.

"Why? It's a big bed. We'll both fit."

She hadn't thought about the size of the bed. Nor seen it. She was still wrapped completely in his arms.

"If it were dark, it would be better," she said.

"Then we'd only have to turn on the light."

"What?"

"I want to see you, Mandy, touch every inch of you, kiss every inch of you. See the pink of your cheeks, the blue of your eyes, feel the silky softness of your hair against me."

"You'll be disappointed, I'm so fat."

"Not fat—large with child. There's a difference. And it's you. Whatever you are, whatever you look like, it's all you. And it's you I want."

He kissed her again, slowly unbuttoning the flannel shirt she wore. Slipping it off her shoulders, he pulled her gently to him, as if he couldn't bear to be away from her for long.

Time was suspended. The outside world ceased to exist. There was only Mandy and Jackson in a sensuous world of two, touching, tasting and learning.

She grew warmer, and wished they could open a window to cool down. He took his time, caressing every inch of her body as he'd promised. She also touched him, brushing fingertips lightly over his chest and arms, then reaching down to gently encircle that hardness that promised so much. Learning his shape and strength.

When he finally entered her, it was the most exquisite

sensation of her life. Moving together, breathing hard, they surged to a cataclysmic climax that left Mandy breathless and boneless and floating on billowing clouds of happiness. The myriad sensations that swept through her like a hot, intense wave were unlike anything she'd ever experienced. Could it last forever?

Their breathing began to slow. The heat that had threatened to consume her faded. Now she was growing chilly. As if attuned to her thoughts, Jackson reached down and drew the covers over them, cocooning them in the warmth of the blankets and each other. He settled her on her side, still in the circle of his arms, resting his chin on the top of her head.

Mandy closed her eyes, savoring every delightful moment. He was strong, yet had been incredibly gentle. He was big, yet they had fit perfectly.

She was floating in the afterglow, pleased with life in general and today in particular. Could anything get any better? She felt herself drifting to sleep.

Softly he kissed her hair. "Sara," he murmured.

It was like a splash of icy water. Mandy's eyes opened and she drew back.

"*Sara?*" she said, scooting to the side of the bed.

"What?" Jackson leaned up on one elbow. "What are you talking about?"

"You just said 'Sara.' I'm not Sara, I'm Mandy. You can't even keep your women straight!" She almost fell out of the bed, but recovered and stood on the rug, shivering in the cool air as mortification swept through her.

"No I didn't," he said.

Scrambling around for her clothes, she yanked on the shirt, seeking some shelter from his gaze. "You did. I heard it loud and clear." Maybe not loud; he'd murmured it as if he were falling asleep. But that didn't matter.

She'd only been a substitute for the wife he loved so much.

Mandy snatched up her jeans and socks and backed to the door, pain flooding through her. The most amazing, incredible, wonderful experience of her life, and she had been a substitute for a dead woman!

"That's impossible," Jackson said again, climbing out of bed. He didn't seem to mind being nude as he advanced toward her.

"Stay away from me. I was nothing but a substitute for your wife. I can't believe I didn't realize it!" Mandy spun around and ran for the sanctuary of her bedroom, slamming the door and turning the lock with a sharp snick. Leaning against it, she let the tears fall. The searing pain in her chest threatened to rip her in two. Here she thought she was falling in love, and the man in question yearned for another woman.

What a *fool* she'd been! How could she have imagined anyone would be so taken with a fat pregnant woman they'd want to woo her and take her to bed? How could she have been so gullible yet again? Hadn't she learned anything from life?

"Mandy, let me in." Jackson knocked on the door, rattled the knob.

"Go away," she said, hoping he couldn't hear the tears in her voice.

"No. I want to talk to you."

"I don't want to talk to you. I'm packing. I'll be gone as soon as I can."

"No you won't. Where would you go? Open the door."

She pushed away and tried to see through her tears.

She needed to leave. Not only the trailer, but the construction site, Julian—maybe even Colorado. She couldn't stay, not after today.

Panic struck. What would she do without this job? It was highly unlikely anyone would offer her a job this close to her delivery date. She would have no medical coverage, no income—and she still needed every penny she could scrape together. She couldn't lose her job over pride.

The door swung open.

She whirled around. "Get out!" How had he managed to unlock it?

"Not until we talk."

"There's nothing to talk about. I'm not Sara!" She almost screamed the words, the ache in her heart growing. Tears spilled down her cheeks. She hurt all over, and rubbing her aching chest, she tried to glare at him through the shimmering tears.

He stepped inside cautiously, moving closer until he was close enough to reach out and touch her if he wanted.

"I know you are not Sara. There was only you and me in that bed. Only you and me kissing and touching and making love. If I said her name as I was falling asleep, I'm sorry. I wasn't thinking of her. I knew every second it was you in my arms."

Mandy dashed the tears away and tried to hang on to the rage that filled her, if only to hold off the panic.

"Get out."

"Mandy, don't cry. You were not a substitute for Sara. Nor for anyone else."

"You had an itch, I was convenient," she said.

"Wrong. If I wanted to scratch an itch, there are plenty of women out there willing to accommodate me.

I haven't had a woman in three years. You're the first I've been with since...since my wife died. You are uniquely you. Special in your own right. I've wanted you for weeks. Why do you think I went to Pueblo?''

"To check on your precious project.'' She would not be swayed by seductive words.

"To try to escape my growing fascination with a blond secretary who was consuming too much of my mind,'' he replied.

"Well, you won't have that problem again. I'll get out of your life and you can go back to the way you were.''

"I'll never be able to do that again,'' he said, reaching out to brush the tears from her cheek. "Don't cry, Mandy. The last thing I wanted to do was make you cry.''

"Get out,'' she whispered, holding on to a shred of control, longing to buy into his words and fling herself back into his arms. To feel that incredible sense of right and happiness that she'd had for so short a time minutes before. But she'd been burned too often to risk it.

Today had been a mistake. She just hoped she could get over it before the end of time.

"I'll leave, but not until I know you are all right,'' he said raggedly.

"I'm fine.'' She brushed away more tears, holding on to her control for all she was worth. She just wanted him out before she died of utter humiliation!

Jackson turned and left, closing the door softly behind him.

She dropped her clothes and flung herself onto the bed, crying as if her heart was broken, which it very well might be.

Chapter Twelve

Jackson headed back to his bedroom and dressed. He went over every moment of the afternoon, unable to believe he'd called Sara's name. Not after being so wrapped up in Mandy he hadn't known where he ended and she began.

She'd been as hot for him as he'd been for her. Her responses had driven him further than he'd ever expected. The entire afternoon was one he would remember forever—but now it would be tainted. Had he really said Sara's name?

God, how unforgivable.

Especially with someone like Mandy, who didn't have a lot of good memories in her background. Who didn't have the self-confidence a woman would need to weather something like this.

He'd made no promises. She knew he wasn't plan-

ning on a long-term affair, but anyone would be hurt to
be merely a substitute for someone else.

Mandy was nothing like Sara. Maybe he should tell
her that. Prove he couldn't have mixed them up.

He took the picture from the dresser drawer where
he'd put it. Sara's smile had once delighted him. It still
warmed his heart when he looked at her and Sammy.
But they were gone. They had died, but he hadn't. Life
went on.

And sometimes windows opened when doors closed.

With a last look, he replaced it in the drawer. He'd
never forget them. They were an important part of his
life and always would be.

But there was someone else now whom he'd hurt,
and he needed to make amends any way he could.

He pulled the covers over the bed and glanced
around. How could things go so wrong in a heartbeat?

Mandy awoke when nature called. The baby seemed
to be practicing for gymnastic events at the Olympics,
she thought, as she picked out clean clothes and opened
the door a crack. Trying to keep her mind empty of
images and regrets, she listened intently, hearing nothing. She crossed to the bathroom and quickly shut the
door.

The shower felt wonderful. She wished she dared
take another soaking bath, but didn't want to stay that
long. Who knew when Jackson might return?

Dressing, she peered into the mirror, dismayed at her
swollen eyes, the blotchy color of her skin.

Darn, how was she going to ask Jeff about her trailer
repairs looking like this? If anyone saw her, speculation
would run rampant and cause the very gossip and dis-
ruption Jackson had warned against at the onset.

"Serves him right," she muttered.

But she would not deliberately cause havoc on the site. He and Jeff had been good enough to let her stay, to earn more money in these few weeks than she'd ever have earned in Denver.

If she had let her expectations soar, it was her own fault when reality slapped her down. She knew she was not meant for a permanent relationship—marriage and a big family. Today provided another example to hammer the fact home.

When she walked into the living room, she was startled to see Jackson sitting on one of the chairs, staring out the window.

He turned when he heard her.

"Will my trailer be repaired soon?" she asked. Her heart pounded, and her mind tumbled with memories—of how he had kissed her, touched her so gently. The delight they'd shared. She closed down tightly. She dared not go there!

"We need to have an insurance adjuster look at it. But it's unlikely we'll repair it this year. The damage is more severe than we first thought."

She took a deep breath. "I need the trailer."

"We've listened to the long-range weather forecasts and it looks as if we only have another week or two of passable weather to work. There's another storm coming in next week, and another expected immediately after that. They are arctic, so they'll be bringing snow. We'll be working flat out to get as much completed and enclosed before we have to suspend operations. There's no time to fix the trailer."

"I can't stay here," she almost whispered.

"You're safe here, Mandy. I won't touch you again."

She swallowed and looked out the window. Of course

he wouldn't touch her again. There was no need. He'd gotten what he wanted.

"If it makes you feel better, I'll bunk in with Jeff," he offered unexpectedly.

She looked at him again. "That would sure give rise to speculation, wouldn't it?"

He shrugged. "Either way, the men will talk."

"Maybe I should leave altogether."

"We'll only be here another couple of weeks, max. Stay and I'll throw in bonus money."

"For services rendered," she said with an edge in her voice.

A hard light entered his eyes. "For staying until the end. You have straightened out the office and everything is up to date and running smoothly. I'd like to close the year out that way."

Nodding, she turned to walk to the kitchen. Maybe a cup of tea would help. At least it gave her something to do. Awkward hardly described how she felt. Embarrassed, humiliated, mortified came close.

And sad.

And the worst of it was, she still was so very aware of the man. Could still feel herself caught against him in an embrace like no other. Could remember every instant of the afternoon—the good and the bad.

He followed her into the kitchen.

"Want to talk?" Jackson asked.

Mandy shook her head. There was nothing to talk about.

"I'm going out then." He hesitated a moment. "Plan to stay until we close up for the winter. I won't touch you again. We'll be roommates, nothing more."

She nodded, her gaze fixed firmly on the teakettle, as if watching it intently would hasten its boiling.

He waited another moment, then left. Mandy listened to him cross to the front door, open it and go out. With the sound of it closing, she knew she was alone.

In one sense she'd always been alone—from the moment her mother had delivered her to social services. Yet Mandy kept hoping this time would be a magic time.

When was she going to learn?

It was easy enough to avoid Jackson the rest of the day. She took snacks and drinks to her room, climbed into bed and read. Fortifying herself proved unnecessary, for he hadn't returned by the time she went to sleep.

Monday the rain had stopped, though the sky was gray and dreary. Water dripped from the trees as if it were still raining.

Mandy dressed warmly and headed for the office. Either Jackson had not spent the night in the trailer or he'd come in late and left early. She saw no evidence of him while she prepared her breakfast.

Jeff was the only person in the office when she entered. She ignored the twinge of disappointment and went straight to her desk after a murmured good-morning. She was glad she didn't have to face Jackson.

"Sorry about your trailer, Mandy. Jackson said he told you we can't fix it," Jeff said, reaching for his hard hat. "Can you get the rest of your things from it today? We want to have it hauled out of here and down to a repair shop before the weather gets any worse. The insurance adjuster will be coming out tomorrow to examine it. After that, we'll leave it in Julian until spring."

"Sure."

He hesitated at the door. "I'm needed outside. Are you all right?"

She nodded and smiled, trying to convey the image of a woman who had everything going just the way she wanted in life.

"Did Jackson tell you we're down to the wire now? Only another two weeks left and we'll close for the winter."

She nodded again, her smile feeling tight and phony. Couldn't he tell?

"You all right with that? We thought we might get more time in."

"It'll give me plenty of time to find an apartment and settle somewhere before the baby comes. Anything special you want me to do today?"

"Just keep on doing what you've been doing."

When Jeff left, Mandy sat back in her chair. Two weeks. In two weeks they'd all go their separate ways. Would she ever see Jackson Witt after that?

She expected him to stay away from her after his actions of yesterday afternoon, so Mandy was surprised that evening when he entered the trailer shortly after she had begun to prepare dinner. She had set a stew to simmering during her long lunch break, running across several times in the afternoon to check on it.

She had just put cornbread into the oven when he arrived.

"Something smells good," he said easily. But the wary look in his eyes belied his casual tone.

"I fixed a stew and have cornbread baking. It'll be ready soon if you want some." There was plenty if he chose to join her. If he refused, she could reheat leftovers later in the week.

"Do I have time enough for a shower?"

She nodded, taking a slow breath. Maybe they could coexist for the next couple of weeks.

Mandy was surprised at the degree of contentment his arrival induced. She still felt raw from yesterday, but a part of her wanted to be with him, no matter what the cost.

Dinner consisted entirely of casual conversation that could have been held between total strangers. Jackson never came near enough to even accidentally brush against her. Never said a word that the entire world couldn't have heard.

And as soon as they were finished, he headed back out, claiming he had work to do at the office. That set the pattern for the week. He was gone every morning before she awoke, and after a hasty dinner, disappeared each evening.

Mandy did her best to keep to her room when he was around, but felt more lonely than before.

On Friday, she had another appointment with her new doctor. She left for Julian right after lunch, driving carefully on the gravel road into town. Evidence of the storm was everywhere. In one spot a tree that had fallen across the road had had the center cut out to allow traffic to pass, both ends still lying on the roadsides. There were puddles in the ruts, and more mud than she remembered.

Still, the trip proved uneventful. Once her appointment was concluded, she headed for the only general merchandise store in town.

She hadn't bought anything for her baby and wanted to get an idea of what was available and how much it all cost.

Wandering through the small department, Mandy was enchanted with the tiny garments, the fancy dresses for little girls and the miniature jeans for boys. What would her baby be? Girl or boy?

The prices concerned her a bit. A crib wasn't cheap, yet it was necessary. Some of the little jumpsuits and sleepers were inexpensive, but she knew babies grew fast.

It was the teddy bear that captured her fancy, so soft, floppy and cuddly that she couldn't resist. It seemed extravagant to purchase a toy when the baby needed more practical things. But she bought it, anyway. Life was not all about practicality.

When she left the shop, she debated about driving home or stopping to eat dinner first. Eating would mean she'd be driving home in the dark on that barely passable road. Yet she wanted pizza. She hadn't had any in weeks and loved it. Pregnant women had cravings. Hers hadn't been outrageous, but she wanted pizza tonight! She would indulge her craving as soon as she put her packages in the trunk.

She almost jumped when she saw Jackson leaning against the side of her car, his arms folded across his chest, his gaze fixed firmly on her as she walked toward him.

She slowed her pace, uncertain what he was doing here.

"Hi," she said when she reached him.

"What do you think you're doing, driving here by yourself?"

Irritation rose. "I'm perfectly capable of driving myself to Julian. It's none of your business."

"I could have brought you in. I'll follow you home."

"I don't need a keeper, Jackson," she said, oddly touched that, despite everything, he'd come after her to make sure she was safe.

"Apparently you do." He stepped aside to let her into the car.

"I'm not going home yet. I'm going to have dinner here in town."

"I'll wait."

She stared at him, and his implacable expression let her know that's exactly what he would do. He could be so stubborn.

But so could she.

"Actually, I'm going for pizza," she said finally. "Do you want pizza for dinner?" It wasn't quite an invitation, but it was the best she could do. She still heard Sara's name on his lips echoing in her mind.

He hesitated a moment. Mandy's heart dropped. No, he didn't want to have dinner with her.

"Pizza sounds good." He glanced up the street and spotted the local pizza parlor. "That place?"

"The only one in town, I think."

They walked up the sidewalk. The shopping bag hung from her fingers. She should have stowed it.

When they entered the restaurant, it was too early for the Friday night crowd. There were booths along one wall, picnic-style tables down the middle with bench seats. Only a few families and couples were present.

"Booth?" Jackson asked.

Mandy nodded and led the way to the first empty one. She slid in one side and he slid into the other. They studied the posted menu on the far wall and decided on a combination pizza. Jackson went to order and returned with a pitcher of cola and two glasses.

"I assumed no beer," he said as he sat back down.

"Not for me."

"Me, neither." He poured their drinks. Silence descended.

Jackson studied her as she looked around. Looked every where but at him, actually. He noticed the bag beside her.

"What did you buy?" he asked.

She glanced at him almost shyly, a small smile lighting her features. Pulling out the brown floppy bear, she sat it on the table. "A teddy bear for the baby. Isn't it darling?"

She gazed at the toy as if it was the most precious thing in creation. Jackson could envision her looking at her baby the same way.

He felt as if he'd been kicked in the gut with a steel-toed work boot. Mandy was the sweetest woman he'd ever met. He'd kissed her, tasted her sweetness, felt every inch of that incredibly soft, womanly body. Their making love had been unforgettable. He wanted her again. Wanted her to look at him with that same gaze she gave a teddy bear.

How could he have hurt her so badly? What could he do to make up for it? He almost ached to reach across and touch her. To have her smile at him. To have her want to touch him back.

Her vulnerability hit him square in the chest. She was alone in the world, with no family, no close friends he'd seen evidence of. Yet she was looking forward to her baby, and to making a home.

"It's foolish, I know, to buy a teddy bear before the baby is even born. And who knows how long it'll be before he or she can play with it? But I couldn't resist."

"How about other things?"

"I looked at them." Some of the delight went out of her face. "Everything's more expensive than I expected."

"Probably here in Julian—they have to pay more to

have it shipped in. You should shop in other places, find a discount house with better bargains.''

She nodded, replacing the bear in the bag.

Jackson hesitated a long moment, then slowly said, ''Sammy's crib is still at my folks'. You could have that if you want.'' He stared at her stunned expression, feeling stunned himself. How could he offer his son's crib to a stranger?

Not a stranger. Mandy.

''Are you sure?''

He nodded. ''We could go there this weekend and pick it up.'' Where had that come from? He hadn't been back to Fort Collins since he'd sold his house and left for that first remote job site, three years ago. He'd never intended to return.

She stared at him warily. ''Fort Collins is clear across the state, almost in Wyoming.''

''I know where it is,'' he replied calmly. His manner belied the sudden tension ratcheting up inside him. Was he crazy? He hadn't been home in years. Was he up to facing Fort Collins and all its memories?

''It would take all day to get there, and all day back,'' she said.

He should take that as an out. But he didn't.

''That's right. We'll head out tomorrow, stay Sunday and return on Monday.''

Mandy started to say something just as his name rang out from the serving counter. Jackson rose and went to get their pizza. He snagged two plates and a few packets of hot sauce. Had he lost his mind? The last thing he wanted to do was return to Fort Collins.

Yet he couldn't stand seeing Mandy distressed. And it had nothing to do with his own part in insulting her after they'd made love. He wanted to help her. Wanted to make things easier if he could. She could use a few breaks in life.

When he placed the pizza on the table, she looked up at him, wariness still evident in her gaze. "Then I say thank-you. I appreciate it. But maybe we ought to wait until I decide on a place to live first. No sense bringing the crib here if I decide to settle back in Denver."

"I don't know how long the roads will be clear. Better to go tomorrow."

She hesitated only a moment, then nodded. "Okay."

They ate the pizza with gusto. Mandy darted puzzled glances at him from time to time, as if she wasn't sure she'd heard him correctly.

No wonder, he thought. Normally he didn't do things so spontaneously. Maybe that's what his life needed these days—more spontaneity.

"We'll have to take my truck," he said, "so we can carry the crib back."

She nodded.

"I'll call my folks. We'll stay with them."

She widened her eyes at that. "Should I? I could get a motel room somewhere."

"Why would you do that?"

"Won't they think it odd, you showing up with me?" After what happened? She didn't say it aloud, but it hung in the air nonetheless.

He looked at the piece of pizza he was about to eat and shrugged. "They probably will be so glad to see me they won't care who is with me." He glanced up. "I didn't mean that quite as it came out. You'll be welcomed."

She didn't want to talk about that night. And he really

had no excuse to offer. Maybe this would ease the hurt he'd inflicted.

Of course, the penance might be more than he could bear. For the first time he thought of what returning to Fort Collins would mean. He hadn't been back since that awful time. Would things have changed? Or look the same, be the same except for the loss of Sara and Sammy?

Jackson led the way back to the construction site. Mandy was glad for the bright headlights filling the road ahead. She stayed close, grateful the man had come, after all.

When they parked their vehicles, Jeff came from his trailer.

"Where have you two been?" he called, walking over.

"Had dinner in town," Jackson said. He opened the door to his trailer and motioned them both in. Mandy passed so close she could feel the heat from his body.

Feeling slightly shaken, she lifted the bag. "I'll put this away." Escaping to her room, she was glad for the brief respite.

Shedding her jacket, she hung it up and took the teddy bear from the bag, setting it on her bed. Smiling, she recaptured some of the happiness she'd had shopping. When she turned to rejoin the men, Jeff's voice stopped her in her doorway.

"What do you mean, you're going to Fort Collins? You haven't been there since Sara died."

"Mandy needs a crib, and Sammy's is at my folks' place. I'm giving it to her."

"Jackson, we have two weeks before we close down. There's too much to do. You can't just take off for three days."

"You can handle it."

"Why now? Why not later?"

"You said it yourself. In two weeks we close down. I'm heading for Boulder and that project until it's completed. Mandy will be off somewhere else. When would I get it for her?"

"Anytime after the next two weeks. Hell, I'll go up and get it then."

"I don't expect to see her again after we close up for winter," Jackson said firmly. "We're going tomorrow."

Mandy crossed her arms over her chest, hugging herself in disappointment. Stupid, she chided herself. Had she thought that, just because he'd offered her the crib, anything had changed?

No wonder he wanted to go so soon. He wanted nothing to extend their time together. In two weeks they'd say goodbye, and that would be that.

She should refuse to go. Tell him she'd changed her mind, that she didn't need anything from him and would manage fine on her own. His first duty was to the job, not to his temporary secretary.

But cribs were expensive.

And this one would be a tie to Jackson.

She turned and slowly closed the door, too dispirited to face the men, after all. Maybe things would look different in the morning. And she had until then to tell Jackson she couldn't go.

It was still dark when Jackson pounded on her door the next morning. Mandy woke and sat up. Was there an emergency?

"Yes?"

He opened the door and stuck his head in, the light from the hall providing illumination.

"We didn't decide what time to leave, but I wanted an early start. Can you be ready to go soon?"

She opened her mouth to tell him she wasn't going, after all. He didn't wait for an answer, but pulled the door shut quickly.

Two seconds later Mandy jumped from the bed and switched on the light. Okay, decision made. She'd go. She needed the crib and he wouldn't have offered if he didn't want her to have it.

And, she admitted, she wanted to spend time with Jackson. They had only two more weeks. Wouldn't she be an idiot to give up a moment with him before she had to?

They were on the road within the hour, after eating a quick breakfast. Mandy had dressed in record time and thrown a few things into a suitcase, which Jackson put in the back of the truck cab. She still wasn't sure she should be going off for the entire weekend with the man.

"We'll stop somewhere along the way for a snack and lunch," he said as they climbed the hill from the construction site.

"We'll be stopping more than that," she murmured, glancing at him to judge his reaction.

He laughed. Mandy's heart skipped a beat. He was so gorgeous when he smiled. She'd seen him laugh only a couple of times. It always changed his features until she thought him the most beautiful thing she'd ever seen. She tried to imprint every detail of his face on her mind. She never wanted to forget Jackson Witt.

"I know about pregnant women and their bathroom needs," he said. "Just let me know when."

She nodded, not feeling embarrassed as she'd thought she might.

"I called my folks last night to let them know to expect us. They weren't home. I tried a neighbor and found out they're gone for the weekend," Jackson said casually. "I thought they'd be home."

"Oh."

He flicked her a quick glance but didn't say anything more.

Mandy gazed out the window, wondering why, after staying in his trailer with him for over a week, the thought of going to his family home unchaperoned made her feel so daring. It wasn't as if there was anything between them. Just her own awareness and yearnings. But he'd proved she didn't mean a thing to him.

Jackson was still in love with his dead wife.

It was slow going along the curvy mountain roads, but once they reached the interstate, they made good time, despite Mandy's request to stop every couple of hours. It was dinnertime and already growing dark by the time they headed into Fort Collins.

Mandy was aware of the tension rising as Jackson slowly drove into town. She looked at him, but his gaze was firmly fixed on the road in front of them.

She didn't say a word until he pulled into a driveway and cut the motor.

From what she could see in the waning daylight, the house was a nice ranch style in a lovely older neighborhood. Tall trees lined the streets, and the lawns were wide and nicely kept.

"This is it," he said.

"You grew up here?"

He nodded. "My folks bought this when Randy was just a baby." He looked at her. "He's my older brother, lives in Alaska.'' Slowly Jackson raised his gaze and looked around, the tension seeping away.

''Let's unload, freshen up and go for dinner.''

Mandy nodded in agreement. It couldn't be easy for Jackson to be here. Maybe he'd want to leave first thing in the morning. If his parents weren't home, there was no reason for him to stay in Fort Collins beyond picking up the crib.

The house was comfortably furnished. As he showed her to a bedroom, Mandy glanced around, noticing the plush sofa that looked as if it called to be sat on. A wide-screen TV sat against the wall, beside a stereo system that looked state of the art. Pictures on the walls gave the place a homey feeling.

The room he showed her to was obviously a guest room—impersonal, yet furnished with everything a visitor would need.

''The bath is across the hall. My room is next door. This was Randy's. Mom changed both of the rooms when we moved out.''

''So no teenage memorabilia?'' she teased.

''Packed in the garage. Wait until you see it. The place would put the Smithsonian to shame. She has her dolls from when she was a kid, and some old toys of Dad's that Grandma gave her. Plus all my stuff and Randy's. Mom never throws anything away.''

Mandy smiled wistfully. She had nothing from when she'd been little, not even clear memories of her mother. Did Jackson have any idea how lucky he was?

Chapter Thirteen

"I'll be ready in a few minutes," she said, stepping inside the lovely room and firmly pushing away the wistful yearnings that rose.

"Take your time. I'll be in the living room when you're ready."

She put her overnight case on the small chair near the window and opened it. She hung up the shirts, put the jeans in the drawer and arranged her cosmetics on the dresser. She brushed her hair, going to stand by the window.

The backyard must have been a child's dream. Huge old trees provided limbs for a swing and tree house. Peering closely, she saw there was indeed a platform nestled in the sturdy branches. From when the boys were young, she knew. A pang of regret struck her.

She wished she had more to offer her baby—a history of a loving family going back generations. Places they could visit that held meaning. People who had known her all her life.

Instead, it would be Mandy and her baby against the world.

"Not to worry, little one," she said, rubbing her tummy gently. "We'll make our own traditions and make memories to last a lifetime."

When she walked into the living room, Jackson was standing at the big window, staring out.

"Are you all right?" she asked.

He turned and nodded. "Just thinking."

"Jeff said once you hadn't been home in three years. Do you want to leave in the morning?"

He hesitated a moment, then slowly shook his head. "I want to show you around Fort Collins. You might like it here, might want to settle here instead of in Julian. It's still got a small-town atmosphere, but has more to offer than Julian, and it's a lot closer to Denver."

Settle in the one place Jackson avoided? She didn't think so. Not that he'd come back to Julian, but she could always hope. She smiled and shrugged her shoulders.

"Come on, let's go find something to eat," he suggested. "What would you like?"

"Anything, as long as there's a lot of it. I'm starved."

Mandy was trying to recapture the feeling of friendship that had begun before their disastrous night together. Jackson seemed to be trying, as well. She wouldn't think about what might have been, but concentrate on what was.

He took her to a family restaurant a block off the main street. It served a wide assortment of entrées. She chose baked ham, while Jackson chose rare steak.

"So tell me all about growing up in Fort Collins," she invited when their food arrived.

"It's a good place for kids, safe." Then, as if he realized what he'd said, and how his own son had died, he stopped. "Most of the time, that is. It was when I was growing up."

"And it should have been for your son. I'm sorry," she said, feeling the helpless frustration of being able to do nothing to ease his pain.

"A random act of violence. Fort Collins is a great place, still safe for children."

"So if I settled here, where should I look? Your parents' neighborhood would be too expensive on a secretary's salary. Always supposing I could get a job in a few months."

"I know some people in town. I can put in a good word," he said.

She nodded, once again feeling disappointment. Why did she keep hoping for more than came her way? What had she expected him to say—no need to worry, you'll have a job with us in the spring?

Yes, that was exactly what she'd wanted him to say!

"The Cutter Hill section is nice. Lots of apartment buildings there, and the schools are good. We could drive over there tomorrow, if you like. So you could see the area."

"I would, thank you," she said.

Slowly Jackson began to speak of things he and his brother had done as children. Of the freedom they'd enjoyed once they had bikes. Of Randy's getting a car when he was sixteen and how he'd let Jackson ride around with him despite some of the protests of his cool friends. When Jackson got his license, Randy had even let him borrow it—until he got his own wheels.

She laughed at the way Jackson portrayed their constant battles to keep those old clunkers running, and the two times he'd gotten a ticket and had his father come down on him.

Jackson spoke of fishing and skiing and family vacations.

Mandy soaked it all in. To her, it sounded like the perfect life for a child. Just like the one she wanted her own baby to be able to look back on.

"Denver was different, I bet," he said perceptively at one point.

She nodded. "And not having one family to grow up with sure puts a different spin on things."

He reached out and took her hand. Mandy went still, startled by the tingling sensations racing through her. He didn't mean anything to her. She couldn't let Jackson mean anything.

But he did, and idiot that she was, she cherished every moment spent with him, relished every touch. She met his gaze and almost caught her breath when she saw his expression.

She didn't know whether to wish she'd never met Jackson Witt or wish he would never let her go.

"Neither of us can change the past, but we have to go on. You'll be a wonderful mother to your baby, and be able to give it a great life."

Her heart melted. "Thank you." She let her hand stay in his, wishing he'd pull her into his arms, kiss her and hold her so tightly she could imagine he'd never let her go.

But he merely squeezed her hand slightly and released it.

By the time they returned home, Mandy had her emotions firmly under control.

"Thanks for dinner," she said. "What time should I get up in the morning?"

"Are you ready for bed so soon? It's not even ten," Jackson said, closing the front door behind him. He leaned on it, crossing his arms and regarding Mandy.

"I'm tired from the drive. But I'll be ready to start early if you want."

He shook his head. "Sleep in as long as you like. The garage will be waiting whenever we get to it."

She bade him a quiet good-night and walked down the hall to the guest bedroom. Sleep proved elusive, however, with so many thoughts of Jackson swirling in her mind.

Jackson awoke early the next morning. It felt odd to be back in the room he'd had as a kid. His mom had changed everything except the placement of the window. He could still see the limbs of the old oak silhouetted against the dawn sky. He and Randy had used that old tree as a fort, for swings, for playing Tarzan.

He had always thought Sammy would enjoy it as much.

Disliking the trend of his thoughts, he rose and showered. Listening by Mandy's door for a moment assured him she was still asleep. He headed for the kitchen. It didn't take long to prepare coffee, and he poured a cup of the hot brew as he gazed out the kitchen window into the backyard. But his thoughts were a long way away from the play area of his childhood.

Rousing himself, he finished the coffee and went for his jacket and car keys. He'd visit the bakery over on Elm Street and get something for breakfast.

The small strip mall that housed the bakery also held a video store, a dry-cleaning establishment and a florist.

The clerk at the flower store was setting out buckets of fresh flowers when he drove into the parking lot.

He bought an assortment of croissants and sweet rolls, not knowing what Mandy might like. On his way back to the car, he hesitated, eyeing the flowers.

Ten minutes later Jackson turned slowly into the gravel driveway of the cemetery. It was deserted this early on a Sunday morning. Frost still dusted the grass, and the trees, denuded of their leaves, looked bleak. He stopped and climbed out, picking up the two bouquets.

Walking toward the monument he recognized, he was surprised to see that the earth wasn't raw and red, but grass had covered the places his loved ones lay.

Flowers just past their prime were in the containers by the headstones. Someone had been there recently.

Suddenly he felt guilty. He'd avoided coming for three years, while others had visited.

"Hi, Sara," he said softly, pulling out the wilting flowers and putting the bouquet of red roses into the vase. There was still some water in it. He had nothing else to say. She wasn't here. Her laughter danced on the wind. Her smile warmed his heart, but never again would he see it on her face. Her touch was but a memory. The searing pain he expected was missing. Poignant memories flooded, but they were of happy times. They had had a lot of happy times.

He moved to the tombstone next to hers. The little lamb on top would have pleased Sammy, Jackson thought, placing the bouquet of daisies and carnations in the holder. A kid would like daisies, he thought, brushing the lamb gently. Maybe it should have been a puppy. Sammy had wanted a puppy so badly. Jackson and Sara had decided that when he was a little older they'd get a dog.

Jackson wished they'd bought it that summer.

Swallowing hard, his eyes filling with tears, he gazed down at the ground. He missed them. He loved them.

Time to move on.

He blinked and took a deep breath. It was time to move on. Neither Sara nor Sammy would have wanted him, or anyone, to grieve forever.

And he had moved on. He had a good job, a few friends. All he needed.

What about love and laughter?

The words seemed whispered on the wind.

He touched Sara's tombstone and turned to walk away. Coming here hadn't been as hard as he'd thought. He would never again fear to visit. The initial pain had faded, just as his mom had said it would. Now only the familiar ache remained.

When Jackson entered the kitchen, Mandy was sipping a cup of tea. She looked at him warily.

"I went to get breakfast," he said, holding up the white bag. "And to the cemetery."

"Oh, Jackson." She rose and came to his side, reaching for his hand and squeezing it gently. "That must have been hard." Her eyes were bright with sympathy, her voice soothing.

"Not as hard as I thought it would be." He took a breath, threading his fingers through Mandy's and holding on. "They've been gone a long time, and life moves on."

She nodded, her warmth just what he needed to dispel the cold.

"Hungry?" he asked.

"As ever." Slowly she pulled her hand away. "Is the coffee still good? Or shall I make some fresh?"

"It'll be fine. I bought an assortment of things, didn't

know what you'd like.'' He dumped the contents of the bag on a plate and pushed it into the middle of the table—croissants, muffins, rolls and cinnamon buns.

"This is nice," she said, choosing a croissant. "I'm sorry I didn't get to meet your parents."

He nodded in acknowledgment. "Did you ever try to find your parents once you were grown?" he asked. He'd been thinking more and more about her childhood as he compared his own to hers.

She shook her head. "I thought about it. I fantasized about both parents finding me, that they'd been searching for me ever since I was little." She looked into his eyes. "I pretended they'd known they'd made a mistake and were trying to rectify it." She shrugged and broke off a bit of pastry. "But it was a kid's fantasy. They knew what they were doing. If they didn't want me, I didn't want to know them. So I never looked."

"They missed a lot," he said softly.

She beamed at him. "Jackson, that's the nicest thing anyone has ever said to me!"

He frowned, balled up his napkin and rose. "It's true. You ready to tackle the garage? I don't know where the crib will be. We might have to move half the contents to get to it. Wait until you see the stuff Mom keeps."

"I stand ready to help!" Mandy said, jumping up and clearing their dishes.

"Leave those until later. And I don't need help. You shouldn't be lifting or pushing anything heavy."

"Yes sir!" She snapped a sassy salute.

Jackson felt a stir of desire at the laughter on her face. She was so pretty. Did she know that? He didn't think she had a clue. He ached at the thought of a lonely little girl always hoping her parents would come for her. Life was unfair too often.

Turning before he could get caught up in her laughter, he headed for the garage.

Mandy put on her jacket and followed.

Jackson raised the large door to allow more light and make space to move things around. He sighed when he looked at all the boxes and pieces of furniture his mother had saved.

"Wow," Mandy said from beside him, peering into the crammed garage.

"She could probably supply the needs of a small third-world country with what she has here," he muttered, stepping in.

He tugged and pushed boxes around, stacking some on the driveway. Mandy read the labels and wondered at all the things Jackson's mother had deemed worthy of saving.

"Here it is," he called. Two more trips carrying boxes, and then he brought out the frame of a crib. It was wrapped in a sheet, which Jackson stripped away. The oak finish was in perfect condition, the spindles set close together to prevent a baby's head from getting caught. He leaned it against a stack of boxes and went back in. A moment later he returned with the mattress and springs. The mattress had been wrapped in plastic, but the springs were dusty.

A car drove down the street and pulled into the driveway, stopping at the stack of boxes. Jackson looked up, then went on alert.

What was George Andrews doing here? Had he come to see Jackson's parents? Or had he learned Jackson was in town?

Mandy stepped closer. "Company?"

"Sara's father."

The older man climbed from the sedan and glanced

around, his eyes fastening on Mandy for a long moment. He looked at Jackson, questions in his eyes.

"It's been a while, son," he said.

Jackson nodded, but didn't move forward to greet his former father-in-law. The embezzlement by his son stood in their way.

George closed the distance and held out his hand.

Jackson gripped it in greeting.

The older man looked at Mandy. "Your mother didn't tell me you had remarried."

Jackson frowned. "I haven't. This is Mandy Parkerson. She's...a friend."

Mandy smiled politely.

The older man nodded, then turned back to Jackson. "I need to talk to you, son."

Jackson knew what was coming and didn't want to deal with it. "About Marshal?"

George nodded. "Maybe we could go inside and discuss the matter." He flicked a glance at Mandy.

"Mandy knows all about it. She's my secretary at the construction site." Jackson did not say she'd been the one to discover the discrepancies. It didn't change anything.

"Things have been tough since Sara died. We need to discuss how to handle the situation. Family should stick together in hard times. Sara would have wanted that," the older man said.

"Sara would not have condoned theft," Jackson said evenly.

George flinched, hesitated, then nodded. "You're right. But she would have wanted to help her brother."

"It's out of my hands."

"But you could say something to mitigate the

charges. Hell, I'll pay back the money. You won't be out a dime.''

''It isn't me calling the shots. J&J Construction and Windhaven are the ultimate victims. And neither is giving any ground.''

''Family always came first with Sara. She'd want you to help out here, Jackson. She'd be disappointed in you.''

Jackson nodded slowly. ''I think you're right. And I plan to change that. But not by helping Marshal.''

''What are you talking about?''

''I can't do anything for Marshal. He embezzled the money, got caught, has to pay the piper. But I can stop living my life as if it stopped the same time Sara's and Sammy's did. That's where I think she would have been disappointed in me.''

George shook his head. ''I had hoped for better from you.''

''Sorry, I can't compromise on what's right,'' Jackson said in a hard voice.

The older man frowned and turned abruptly, heading for his car without another word.

When the car was gone, Mandy looked at the man standing beside her. He seemed so alone.

''Sara would have been proud that you stood up for what was right,'' she said.

He looked at her. ''You think?''

She nodded. ''Definitely.''

''You never met her.''

''Doesn't matter. I know you, so I can imagine the kind of woman you'd marry.''

''She always fought injustice, and I think letting someone get away with a crime would be the height of injustice.''

* * *

Mandy wished Sara's father hadn't come. They'd been enjoying the morning, talking easily as Jackson moved boxes. Now he seemed to withdraw.

"Let's get the crib in the truck," he said, reaching for the springs.

When it had been loaded, he turned back to the garage, bypassing the boxes stacked on the driveway. A moment later, he came out with another large cardboard box. Placing it on top of two others, he ripped off the sealing tape.

Opening it, he gestured to Mandy. She peered inside. Neatly folded baby clothes.

"Oh, aren't they sweet?" She drew one sleeper from the stack. It was so small. She held it up and smiled. "Hard to imagine a baby would fit in this, isn't it?"

He nodded, staring at the sleeper.

She folded it and put it back, looking at Jackson, then at the box of baby clothes. Sammy's, obviously. Why had he brought it out?

"They're from the first year, I think. If you can use them, you can have them."

"Oh, I couldn't."

"Why not?"

"Don't you want them?"

"I don't need baby clothes. And they don't hold any special memories. Unlike my mother, I don't save everything that ever passed through my life."

"But one day you might want them...."

He studied her for a moment, then shook his head. "No, I won't."

Mandy knew from Jeff that Jackson didn't plan to ever marry again, but still, what if something happened and he changed his mind?

"Thank you," she said. She wouldn't look for problems. He'd offered, and Lord knew she could use them. Gently she rubbed her fingertips over the soft cotton.

"We can take the box inside and you can look at all the different outfits, decide if you don't want some."

"I'd love to see every one." But she knew she'd take them all. The quality was good. Babies outgrew clothes the first year long before they could be worn out.

When her baby outgrew the outfits, she could pass them on. Or save them, in case Jackson ever wanted them back.

He carried the box inside and left Mandy with it while he went to restack the other boxes in the garage. She drew out sleepers and gowns, receiving blankets and sheets for the crib. She separated the piles and fingered the dainty clothes with excitement. Soon her own baby would be wearing these things. She or he would kick her or his legs in the sleepers, wear the corduroy crawlers, the striped T-shirts. There were few things specifically for a boy. Almost everything could be worn by a girl just as easily. Granted, there were no dresses, and if she had a little girl, Mandy would want to dress her up once in a while. But this was such a boon. Jackson had saved her a lot of money, plus indecision about what to get.

Now she needed only to find a place to live, get the nursery set up and prepare for her baby's arrival.

Mandy napped after lunch. Once she awoke, Jackson suggested they drive around Fort Collins.

"I'll start with the Cutter Hill section. I think you'd fit in there," he said as they climbed into the truck.

"Will the crib be okay in back?"

"It can't fall out, and no one will take it."

They drove through the downtown area, then out to

the different neighborhoods of Fort Collins. It was a pretty town. Mandy knew it would look even lovelier in the summer when all the trees were in full leaf and flowers bloomed in gardens. Maybe she should consider living here.

"Thank you for showing me around," she said at one point in the afternoon. "I know this can't be easy for you."

"Why not? It's my hometown."

"I know, but you haven't been here in three years."

He reflected a moment. "True. I thought it would be too hard. But it's not. I have a lot of good memories."

Just then they turned the corner and he stopped at the side of the road, looking at a brick elementary school.

"That's where a crazed man killed five people." He stared at it for a long time. "I never considered how hard it must have been for all those children who saw the killings to return to school. For the teachers to resume their teaching." He was silent for a long moment.

"It's just a building, not an evil spot in the world. A tragic thing happened there, but it was over in seconds. And lightning never strikes in the same place twice. It's probably the safest school in the country," he said at last.

Mandy touched his hand, moved when he gripped hers hard in return.

"Let's go find something to eat. I'm hungry," she said. She wanted to leave the school. Wanted Jackson to leave the terrible memories behind.

They ate at a Mexican restaurant that Jackson said was a favorite. The music was loud and they almost had to shout to be heard—until he moved from across the table to the chair next to hers. Bending their heads close together, they could talk without the need to yell.

Mandy felt the familiar flutter when he leaned near. She longed to reach out and touch him. Twice when she'd offered comfort, he'd latched on to her hand, not rebuffed her as she'd feared he might.

But she wanted more than that.

And knew better than to tempt fate.

Dinner turned out better than she had anticipated. Jackson seemed happier than anytime she'd seen him. It didn't seem as if the weight of the world sat on his shoulders.

Had coming to Fort Collins banished some of his ghosts?

They listened to the band play for a while, then mutually agreed it was time to go home.

When they entered the house, Jackson closed the door and looked at her.

"Thanks again," she said brightly. "That was the best meal I've had in ages."

"And you ate enough for two," he teased.

She laughed. "So maybe the baby will grow up with a true appreciation of good Mexican food! Good night."

"Do you have to go to bed right away?"

Mandy was taken aback. "Um, I'm a little tired."

"Too sleepy for something to drink?"

"Oh, well, not sleepy, exactly." She hesitated, mesmerized by the glint in his eye.

"I could fix you some herbal tea," he offered, stepping closer, reaching out to unbutton her jacket.

Mandy couldn't have moved a step if the house collapsed around them. She was caught in Jackson's direct gaze, caught up in the air of anticipation that seemed to cloud her mind.

"That would be nice," she said as she slipped the jacket from her shoulders when he tugged.

He shrugged out of his, dropping both on the floor.

Slowly his head lowered until his lips touched hers, his hands threading through her hair. Giving a sigh, Mandy leaned closer, into the kiss she knew she should never accept.

His arms came around her and pulled her against him until she was pressed to his hard frame.

Her own arms seemed to have a life of their own as they encircled his neck, tugging him closer, reveling in the heat that spread like wildfire.

When he deepened the kiss, she forgot about the last time, forgot the hurt, remembered only the glorious feelings that filled her when Jackson made love to her.

He pulled back slightly, gazing down into her starry eyes. "I want you, Mandy. Only you, no one else."

Chapter Fourteen

Mandy's heart thrummed in her chest, the blood pounding so hard through her veins she could scarcely hear. But she heard what he said and knew what he meant.

"Tonight it's you and me, no one else, never anyone else," he said, kissing her again.

She felt as if the house whirled around, but it was Jackson picking her up and carrying her down the hall to his room. Laying her gently on the twin bed, he placed one knee beside her, leaning over her, his hands threading through her hair.

"Says it's all right, Mandy. Say you want me as much as I want you."

"Yes." It was all she could say, all she needed to say. The past and future could take care of themselves. Tonight all that mattered was Jackson and her—alone in the world, yet together.

He slowly, almost reverently, undressed her. She reciprocated, reveling in the feel of his taut muscles, of his hot skin. When there was nothing left between them, he lay beside her on the narrow bed, nibbling kisses along her jaw, across her throat, down to her breasts.

''You are so beautiful,'' he whispered, his hands caressing everywhere.

Mandy felt beautiful, just because he said it.

He traced patterns of fire and ice, moving over her, caressing her, bringing her to the brink time and time again, yet stretching out that pleasure until she thought she'd go crazy.

When his fingers tangled in the curly hair at the top of her thighs, he took his time, as if the silky curls intrigued him. His lips traced her jaw, paused at that pulse point at the base of her throat. When she thought she could stand no more, he settled her easily on her side and slid into the heat that waited.

Mandy exploded with feeling as sensations swept through her like a tsunami, filling every cell with pleasure and delight. His own completion followed, rippled through him, making their union complete.

She tried to breathe, but could only pant. She was so hot, yet didn't want to move an inch from the man who had come to mean so much to her. Touching Jackson, loving him, was the most wondrous thing.

Closing her eyes tightly, Mandy held her breath. She couldn't give her heart away again. Not to someone who clearly didn't want a commitment to the future. No one ever stayed, she knew that. This time was no different.

But she feared it was too late. She loved Jackson Witt. Not with the airy romantic love she'd thought she felt for Marc, but with her whole being. She loved spending time with him whether he was in a grumpy mood or not. She liked his dry sense of humor, his dedication to work and to the projects under construction. His integrity.

She especially loved making love with him.

She knew he didn't return her feelings, but she couldn't stop them any more than she could have stopped that tree from falling on her trailer.

She had two weeks left. She'd make the most of them. And when they parted, she'd have a lifetime to remember him, and love him, and wish him well.

He rolled to his side, bringing her half on top of him as he settled them comfortably.

"Could have used a bigger bed," he grumbled.

She giggled softly. "This one's fine."

"Glad my folks aren't home," he muttered a few minutes later.

"Mmm." She just wanted to float in the afterglow, not thinking, not feeling anything but the delight that still saturated her body.

"I never brought anyone home before," he said.

She opened her eyes and gazed up at him. "Never?"

"Not to stay the night."

She nodded, closing her eyes, wishing he hadn't mentioned it. Of course, Sara had lived in Fort Collins. She'd had no reason to come stay the night. Was he ever going to be over her?

"I'm sorry," he said, rubbing his hand slowly up and down her back.

"For what?"

"For saying that. I know what you're thinking. But she doesn't belong here with you and me, Mandy. She's gone."

Mandy nodded again, sighing softly. Sara was not

gone from Jackson's mind and she doubted she ever would be.

Slowly Mandy drifted to sleep, held in the arms of the man she loved.

When Mandy awoke the next morning, she was alone in the bed. She grabbed her clothes, pulling on her shirt, then headed for her room. She took her overnight case into the bathroom with her and proceeded to shower and dress. Once that was done, she packed all her things and carried the case with her. They'd be leaving soon. Where was Jackson?

She found him in the kitchen, coffee already prepared, a plate of bagels and cream cheese on the table.

She hesitated, unsure of morning-after etiquette, then smiled shyly. "Good morning."

He rose at the sound of her voice and turned to her. Sweeping her into a kiss, he made her forget everything for a long moment. Then he let her go and winked.

"We need to get going soon," he said.

"I was surprised you didn't pound on the door at four-thirty and demand we leave then."

"I would have had another way to waken you this morning. But I thought you should sleep as long as you could. It's a long drive back."

"Thanks. I'll eat and be ready to go."

She refused to comment on last night, or their relationship. Did they even have one?

Last night had been special. Stupendous, actually. But nothing had been said about any future.

Two more weeks and they'd go their separate ways. He'd made that clear to Jeff.

But Mandy would always have her memories. If they were bittersweet, they were still all hers nonetheless.

Maybe one day she could tell her baby where the crib had come from, and about the man who meant more to Mandy than anyone ever had.

She made one last bathroom stop before they departed. When she came out, Jackson was on the phone. He hung up.

"That was Jeff. He thought I needed an update before we head back."

"Anything wrong?"

"No. Your trailer's being hauled out this morning. The building inspector showed up at eight—a minor miracle, I'd say. And the road in is drying. Here's hoping the storms hold off for a while."

"But we still need to get back."

"Afraid so. Ready?"

She smiled and nodded, hoping he didn't see the effort it cost her. Things would be different when they returned to the site. He'd be focused on the business at hand. She'd be caught up in trying to decide where to live when the job ended. Their hiatus from real life would be over.

It was dark by the time Jackson eased down the hill to the construction site. He glanced at Mandy. She'd been asleep since their last stop, about fifty miles before Julian. They'd had dinner and she'd complained about being tired. How she could sleep through the bumping of the truck on the access road was beyond him. Obviously she was worn out.

He stopped by his trailer and cut the engine. He was tired, too. Driving all day was as exhausting as working a twelve-hour shift.

He looked at the sleeping woman. How had she come

to mean so much to him in so short a time? He had loved his wife and had sworn never to fall in love again. The pain of losing a loved one was too great.

Yet the protective urge he had around Mandy was as unexpected as it was unwelcome. He didn't want to feel connected with anyone. Despite the walls he'd built, she'd breached them.

He was growing to care. And he didn't like the thought.

"Mandy, we're home." He shook her shoulder.

When she blinked and opened her eyes, he was startled at the warmth that look brought. Frowning, he pushed away the thought.

"Can you manage?" he asked abruptly. The last thing he wanted was to feel anything. Numbness had a price, but it was worth it to keep pain at bay.

"I'm fine. Wow, I slept all the way?" She looked around, opened her door and slid out.

He got out and picked up their cases from the back of the truck, carrying them to the trailer. Seconds later they were inside.

He remembered closing the door to his parents' place and almost jumping her. All through dinner last night he'd wanted her. And her welcome had been genuine.

The same feelings threatened to swamp him again. But he tamped them down. He was not going to become involved in a long-term affair with Mandy Parkerson!

"I'll head for the office, check on any messages. See you in the morning." He dropped their bags and headed out faster than was polite. But he was running for his life.

Jackson felt like a coward, but was unable to deal with the emotions that were threatening to swamp him.

The sooner he got back to work, the sooner things would straighten out and life would go on as it had before Mandy arrived.

The next two days were very much as the week before their trip to Fort Collins had been. Jackson was gone before she awoke in the morning. He stayed away from the office most of each day. Dinner for Mandy on Tuesday was solitary—he ate with Jeff.

On Wednesday, he ate quickly and left almost before finishing the last bite.

Mandy washed the dishes slowly, wondering what had happened. For one special night she'd thought they'd drawn closer.

Now it was as if they were back to square one. If the job wasn't going to end soon, she'd expect him to fire her and get someone else.

Thursday morning, Mandy awoke feeling out of sorts. She dressed slowly. Nothing appealed for breakfast. She settled for a banana and some tea. Heading for the office, she was struck by a pain in her abdomen so intense she doubled over, almost falling onto the dirt.

Stunned, she held her stomach, trying to breathe through the pain. She couldn't be going into labor. It was far too soon. She wasn't close to term. But the gripping pain encircled her back and lower abdomen.

Taking a deep breath, she was able to slowly straighten a moment later. Take another deep breath. Three steps later, another sharp pain hit her, starting at her back and moving around to the front, low down and hard.

She moaned with the intensity, sinking to her knees, holding on and hoping she wouldn't scream.

"Mandy?" Jeff hurried from the office. "Mandy, what is it?"

She looked up. "I'm having sharp pains. I can't go into labor. It's not time! What if something's wrong with the baby? Ohh…'' Another pain. She felt panicky. She couldn't lose her baby!

Jeff scooped her up and carried her to his trailer, rushing inside and placing her gently on the sofa. Two of the men noticed and ran to see if they could assist. He sent them to find Jackson. Dialing the hospital, Jeff talked to Mandy as he waited for someone to answer.

"Hold on, Mandy. We'll figure out the best plan and get moving. You're going to be fine and we're not losing that baby!"

The hospital nurse said she should come in immediately, that they'd send an ambulance if needed. By that time Jackson had arrived. After one look at Mandy, he took the phone from Jeff and spoke sharply. "What do we do?"

When the nurse reiterated the option of sending an ambulance, he spoke again. "No, it'll take twice as long that way. We'll bring her in." He hung up and turned to Jeff. "What happened?"

"She's having pains. Too early for labor."

Jackson crossed swiftly to her and knelt down beside her. "You're going to be okay," he said.

She threw her arms around his neck and clung. "I'm so afraid," she whispered. "Don't let me lose my baby."

"I won't." He picked her up. "Your SUV will be better than the truck," he said to Jeff.

"Let's go."

Jeff drove, and Jackson sat in back with Mandy cradled in his arms. When the pains came, he tightened his grip, feeling helpless as he rubbed his hand along her swollen stomach, crooned meaningless words to try to calm her. He was certain this wasn't a normal part of pregnancy, but he didn't want to scare her any more than she was.

Or than he was.

He longed to shout at Jeff to drive faster, but the man was already pushing it on the gravel road. Still the moments ticked by slowly. Fear clutched Jackson.

Mandy sagged against him, cuddling closer, clinging as if he were her lifeline.

"You're going to be all right, you hear?" Jackson said softly.

"I'm going to hold you to that," she said.

"Ah, Mandy, nothing's going to happen to your baby. You just hang on."

She nodded, closing her eyes. A few moments later another contraction gripped her. Despite his words, Jackson saw the fear in her eyes. He prayed she didn't see it in his.

When they reached Julian's small hospital, Jeff drove directly to the emergency entrance. Jackson carried Mandy inside, where they were met by a nurse who directed them to a nearby cubicle.

A doctor appeared instantly. In seconds, he'd hooked up a fetal monitor and started an IV with medications to stop the contractions. He kept constant, close watch on Mandy for a half hour. Jackson never left her side, holding her hand while she clung as if she'd never let go.

The contractions gradually slowed, grew less severe and finally stopped.

She was exhausted. Closing her eyes, she seemed to drift off to sleep. Jackson gently began to withdraw his hand, but she tightened her grip, her eyes flying open.

"Don't go."

"I'm not going anywhere," he said.

The doctor cleared his throat. "Actually, I want her admitted to ICU until we make sure nothing more is going to happen. We'll take her upstairs and get her settled. You can see her again after that. But for now, I'll have to ask you to wait in the reception area."

Jackson nodded. He leaned over Mandy and brushed her hair back from her face. "I'll see you once you're settled."

She nodded. Jackson's heart was struck at the fear still lingering in her eyes. She tried to smile, but her lips trembled. He kissed her gently, squeezed her hand one last time and turned. He wanted to smash something, rail against fate. Mandy didn't deserve this.

Once outside the curtained area, he stopped, trying to get his emotions under control. He felt as helpless as he had when he'd learned about Sara and Sammy. There should be something a man could do at times like these.

He walked to the reception area. Jeff was sitting with his head bent, elbows resting on his knees, his hands dangling between his legs. He heard Jackson and looked up, standing instantly.

"Is she all right?"

"Yes. But they're moving her to ICU. I told her over and over she won't lose the baby, but I don't know that. What if she does, Jeff? It'll kill her. She wants that baby in the worst way." Jackson rubbed his chest. He wanted to do something!

"It's a small hospital, but up to date. They'll give her the best they've got," Jeff said, gripping Jackson's shoulder.

"What if it's not enough?"

"That's out of our hands, boy."

"She asks for so little. Has had so little in life. She needs this baby."

Jeff nodded, watching Jackson closely. "Maybe you need her," he said.

Jackson looked at him. "What does that mean?"

"Love can come in different ways. You and Sara had a young love, grew up together. But time changes things. It's time you looked around you. You didn't die when Sara did. Maybe it was because more happiness was in store for you."

"I'm not getting mixed up with anyone again!" Jackson reiterated the old litany.

"You already are."

"You're seeing things that aren't there."

"Oh, well, if that's the case, you ready to go back to the site? We can call later and see how she's doing."

Jackson stared at Jeff, ignoring the twinkle in the older man's eye. "Damn it, you know I'm not leaving."

"Because you care about her a lot more than you would if Moose or Bill or one of the other men were here. Deny it all you want to the rest of the world, but don't deny it to yourself."

Jackson swung away and began to pace the small area. Jeff watched him. The minutes ticked by. Finally Jackson went to the admitting desk. They'd had long enough to get Mandy into her room. He wanted to see her, to make sure she was all right. To make sure she wasn't going to lose that baby.

"Mandy Parkerson?" he asked.

The nurse checked the computer monitor. "She's in ICU. Are you a relative?"

Jackson shook his head. "I brought her in. I want to make sure she's all right."

"She's resting. Everything is fine," the nurse said in a soothing tone.

"I want to see her."

"Are you family?"

He shook his head.

"I'm sorry. Only family members are allowed on the ICU floor. When she's moved to the medical ward anyone can visit. If you care to leave a phone number, we can let you know when she's been released from ICU."

"I want to see her now, not in a day or two!" Jackson was not going to be put off by mere technicalities.

"I'm sorry, sir."

Jeff joined him. "Problems?"

Jackson's frustration threatened to erupt. "Only family are allowed in ICU."

Jeff rocked back and looked at the nurse. "Does a fiancé count as family?" he asked.

"Yes. Are you engaged to Ms. Parkerson?" the nurse asked Jackson.

He glanced at Jeff, his lips tightening. Where was his resolve when he needed it? He could walk away. Or run, to avoid becoming entangled with another's life. Avoid the pain and frustration and sadness that life promised.

But he'd also eschew happiness and joy and love.

Who was he kidding? He could no more walk away from Mandy than he could fly to the moon.

"I'm her fiancé," he said.

Jackson paused in the doorway to her room. Mandy was lying on her side, her back to the door. An IV pole held a solution, the tube snaking down to her arm. Was she asleep? He took a deep breath, his heart twisting at how slight she looked in the standard-issue hospital bed.

It wasn't too late. He saw she was doing all right. He could leave with Jeff. Call later to see how she was.

He'd been dumb to tell the admitting nurse they were engaged. Though the longer he thought about it, the more it appealed to him. His lofty ideas of going it alone through life had been destroyed someplace between his week in Pueblo and their last night in Fort Collins.

No matter how he fought against it, he wasn't going to reach that stay-out-of-harm's-way goal he'd set for himself. He needed to know she would be safe, well, happy. He wanted to be the one to make sure she stayed safe, well and happy. He wanted to share her days and her nights. See her baby brought safely into the world. Watch the child grow, and watch Mandy take joy in teaching her baby all a parent had to teach of life's lessons.

For a moment a pang struck as he remembered another little baby, one he'd wanted to teach so much. Sammy's days in the sun had been limited. Mandy's baby had its entire life before it.

And it would need a father.

What if it died young? Jackson frowned, rubbing his chest again. Children were so fragile, so precious.

"What if it lives to be one hundred?" he murmured.

Mandy heard him and turned to look over her shoulder. At the sight of her smile, Jackson's heart released the last trace of hesitation. He loved her. And, dammit, she had better reciprocate.

"Hi," he said, stepping into the room.

"Hi. I thought you and Jeff had left."

"No. Jeff is waiting to hear how you are, then he's heading back to the site. I'm staying."

"Oh, Jackson, there's no need. I'm going to be fine.

The drip is countering whatever caused the contractions. The doctor said he'd watch me closely for the next couple of days. Once things look stable, I'll be released. But I'm not sure I can return to work.''

He lowered the rail on her bed and sat on the side, resting his palm against the swell of her belly.

"So baby wants to come early, impatient little cuss. Don't worry about work.''

Her hand covered his. "You don't have to stay. Go back with Jeff. I know there's a lot to do, and time's short.''

"I hire the best. They can manage without me.''

She grinned. "That's not what you said the other day.''

"So I like to feel important.''

Her smile faded. "You are important,'' she said softly. "Thanks for bringing me in. I'm glad I didn't have to come alone in an ambulance.''

"I don't want you to ever have to do anything alone,'' he said.

"I won't, once the baby comes. As long as it comes when it's supposed to.''

"I was thinking more along the lines of an adult, not just your baby. Maybe you should get married.''

"Oh, yeah, like that's going to happen,'' she scoffed. "Besides, I've sworn off men, don't you remember?''

"So maybe you should consider changing your mind and swearing off every other man in the world.''

"Every *other* man?''

"Except me.''

She stared at him.

He raised her hand to his lips and brushed a kiss across her palm.

"Marry me, Mandy. Let me be your husband, lover, father to your baby. Father to babies of our own."

She blinked and shook her head. "I think the drugs are causing hallucinations."

He tightened his grip. This wasn't easy. And it wasn't going the way he'd thought it would. Why didn't she throw herself into his arms and tell him yes?

Instead her look grew wary. "I thought you loved Sara," she said.

"I did. I think I loved her from the time we were in second grade. But she's gone. I won't lie and say I can forget her. I won't ever do that. But she'll never come between us, I promise you that!"

Mandy tugged on her hand, but he refused to release her.

"I thought you wanted no involvement. That after the project closed for the winter, we'd not see each other again. Wasn't that the reason for the hasty trip to Fort Collins to get the crib? So you wouldn't have to see me after we shut down?"

He nodded, his gaze steadfast and calm. "Or so I thought. But it was as if visiting Fort Collins released me from a prison cell of my own making. It's a nice town where a bad thing happened. But I didn't crash and burn when I went back. In fact, I enjoyed showing you my hometown. I wanted you to like it so you'd settle there. Then when I went home to visit my folks, I could stop by and see you."

"Huh?"

"But today put paid to that notion. I can't wait for occasional visits. I wanted to avoid entanglements. I never wanted to feel the pain losing Sara and Sammy brought. But today was worse. You were in pain, in danger of losing your baby, and I was totally helpless.

I realized then that I was involved, entangled and about as wrapped up as a person could be. I was devastated when Sara died, but you know what? I wouldn't trade the years we did have for anything. I would have given my life for her and Sammy—but I wasn't given that choice. So unless I hie myself off to a monastery, there's no avoiding life—fears, pain, loss and all."

He kissed her hand again and leaned forward until he filled her vision.

"But there's all that joy that also comes with living," he said. "And you bring me an abundant measure of that."

Tears welled up in her eyes. "And the baby? Can you accept my baby, too?"

"Yes, Mandy. I will cherish your baby. Sammy taught me how to be a father. I will be the best dad I can for your baby. Our baby. And maybe we'll have more. Take a chance on me, my love. Marry me."

"Love?" she whispered, touching his cheek with her free hand, her other gripping his tightly.

"I love you, Mandy Parkerson. I want you in my life for as long as either of us has. I'm not going to run off when things get tough. I'd never abandon you or our baby. I just want the chance to love you for all time." He held her gaze with his. She had to say yes!

"Oh, Jackson, I love you so much!" She flung her arm around his neck and pulled him closer to kiss him.

He responded, releasing her hand to enfold her in his arms. She was soft and sweet—and his. Her response had been exactly what he'd hoped for. He loved her. And Mandy loved him.

A monitor sounded. A nurse dashed into the room, stopping when she saw the couple break apart guiltily.

"Heart rate increased dramatically," she said dryly,

coming to take Mandy's pulse. "But I don't think in this instance it's a cause for alarm."

"We're getting married," Mandy said happily.

The nurse raised an eyebrow and glanced at her patient's stomach. "Not a moment too soon," she murmured.

Mandy giggled, exchanging a loving look with Jackson.

"I agree," he said, winking at her.

Epilogue

"Push!" Jackson urged his wife, as he supported her in the birthing room in the Fort Collins hospital. It was a snowy day in early December, the perfect day for a baby to be born.

"I am pushing," she panted, straining to give birth. She rested a moment and looked over her shoulder at the man she loved. "If you don't like the way I'm doing this, you take over," she snapped.

Jackson kissed her cheek. "You're doing perfectly. No one could do better. I'm the coach, remember?"

She pushed as another contraction hit and slowly the baby moved down the birth canal.

"A bouncing baby girl," the doctor said, receiving the infant. She handed her to a nurse, who wrapped the baby in a blanket and laid her on Mandy's stomach. Jackson and Mandy gazed at the tiny girl with a mop of curly brown hair. The baby's eyes opened and she blinked, her little chest rising and falling as she gazed solemnly around.

Jackson reached out a finger and caressed her cheek.

"We have a daughter," he said. "And she's as beautiful as her mother."

"Did you want a son?" Mandy asked, hoping he wouldn't be disappointed.

"Maybe next time." He kissed her gently. "Hello, Mommy."

Next time maybe a boy. Or the time after that. Mandy didn't care. She wanted to fill their home with the laughter of children, and share the rich bounty of love Jackson brought. This precious baby was only the first. They had both agreed on that.

"I love you," she said, tears flowing. How could one woman bear so much happiness?

"I love you, Mandy Witt. You and Melanie Sarah."

She smiled and touched the baby, whom they had already decided would be named for another Sara Witt. Mandy had no fears that Jackson still longed for his first wife. He'd shown her in every way that she was his love, his life and his future.

Jeff was in the waiting room, as were her new in-laws. Everyone awaited word of the new baby. There would be celebration and rejoicing that Jackson and Mandy had a beautiful baby girl.

Mandy fit right in with the Witts, amazed at the closeness of family who loved each other. Amazed at how they welcomed her into their midst.

She was constantly surprised at how easily her husband showed his love. He was still the tough, demanding, no-excuse boss on the job site, but behind their closed door, he was as tender and romantic as any woman could wish.

She glanced up and caught her breath. Would she ever lose this wondrous feeling around him? He leaned over and kissed her. They had restrained themselves to just kisses for several weeks. And there would be several more to go before they could make love again, but she could hardly wait. He thrilled her to her toes, and probably always would.

Jackson brushed the baby's downy hair. "In another year or two, we should try for another one. Maybe a boy next time, what do you think?"

She smiled, her heart filled to bursting. There was no greater gift he could have given her. The past was truly behind them both. The future was bright with promise.

*   *   *   *   *

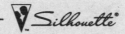

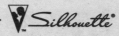

If you enjoyed what you just read,
then we've got an offer you can't resist!

Take 2 bestselling love stories FREE!
Plus get a FREE surprise gift!

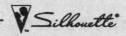

SPECIAL EDITION™

Don't miss the conclusion of
Susan Mallery's
heartwarming miniseries

*They're homegrown, heart-stopping...
and ready to steal your heart!*

Coming in August 2003

QUINN'S WOMAN

Quinn Reynolds has met his match: a woman who
has guts, beauty and who isn't afraid of a challenge.
But Quinn has always kept the world at a distance.
Can this hometown heartbreaker give up his
lone wolf ways and embrace the love of a lifetime?

*Available at your favorite retail outlet.
Only from Silhouette Books!*

Where love comes alive™

It's romantic comedy with a kick
(in a pair of strappy pink heels)!

Introducing

HARLEQUIN®
flipside

"It's chick-lit with the romance and happily-ever-after ending that Harlequin is known for."
—*USA TODAY* bestselling author Millie Criswell, author of *Staying Single*, October 2003

"Even though our heroine may take a few false steps while finding her way, she does it with wit and humor."
—Dorien Kelly, author of *Do-Over*, November 2003

Launching October 2003.
Make sure you pick one up!

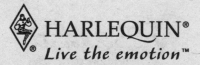
HARLEQUIN®
Live the emotion™

Visit us at www.harlequinflipside.com

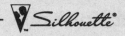

SPECIAL EDITION™

MONTANA MAVERICKS

THE KINGSLEYS
**Nothing is as it seems beneath
the big skies of Montana.**

Return to Rumor, Montana, with

Marry Me...Again
by CHERYL ST.JOHN

Footloose cowboy Devlin Holmes had
wild ways not even marriage could tame...
until his wife decided to leave him.
With their happily-ever-after threatened
by painful mistakes, could he find a way
to honor, cherish and love...again?

On sale August 2003!
Silhouette Special Edition #1558

Only from Silhouette Books!

Where love comes alive™

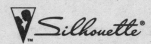
COMING NEXT MONTH

#1555 DANIEL'S DESIRE—Sherryl Woods
The Devaneys

Though he hadn't expected a second chance at happiness, that's exactly what Daniel Devaney got when he came face-to-face with his ex, Molly Creighton. Though a tragic loss had torn them asunder, *this* time Daniel was determined to fight for the love that burned stronger than ever.

#1556 PRINCE AND FUTURE...DAD?—Christine Rimmer
Viking Brides

The princess was pregnant! And the king had every intention of making sure his daughter married the father of her unborn child. But Princess Liv Thorson had other plans, and they didn't include marrying the notorious playboy Prince Finn. Or so she told herself....

#1557 QUINN'S WOMAN—Susan Mallery
Hometown Heartbreakers

Ex-Special Forces agent Quinn Reynolds agreed to share his skills with self-defense instructor D. J. Monroe. But their sessions triggered as many sparks as punches. Fighting the love growing between them might only be a losing battle!

#1558 MARRY ME...AGAIN—Cheryl St.John
Montana Mavericks: The Kingsleys

Ranch foreman Devlin "Devil" Holmes had wild ways not even getting married could tame...until Brynna decided to leave him. Being without her was torture. Could he convince Brynna their marriage deserved a second chance?

#1559 THE FERTILITY FACTOR—Jennifer Mikels
Manhattan Multiples

Nurse Lara Mancini struggled with the possibility that she might be infertile. But her feelings for handsome Dr. Derek Cross were quickly escalating. Would he want to pursue a relationship knowing she might be unable to conceive?

#1560 FOUND IN LOST VALLEY—Laurie Paige
Seven Devils

He wasn't who she thought he was. Seth Dalton, successful attorney, wasn't *really* a Dalton. Amelia Miller was a good woman who deserved a good man, not a fraud. The fact that he was falling for her didn't change a thing...but her love for him— that could be enough to change *everything*.

SSECNM0703